CALCIUM MAGNESIUM AND PHOSPHORUS IN FOOD AND NUTRITION

MAXWELL PRESS

CALCIUM MAGNESIUM AND PHOSPHORUS IN FOOD AND NUTRITION

Henry C. Sherman | Arthur J. Mettler | J. Edwin Sinclair

Department of Chemistry,
Columbia University

MAXWELL PRESS

Chennai   Trichy   New Delhi

MAXWELL PRESS

The edition has been published in india by arrangement with Carson Books, UK

ISBN 978-81-8094-308-9 **Maxwell Press**

All rights reserved No. 44, Nallathambi Street,
Printed and bound in India Triplicane, Chennai 600 005

MJP 980 © Publishers, 2023
Publisher : **C. Janarthanan**

Publisher's Note

The legacy of a country is in its varied cultural heritage, historical literature, developments in the field of economy and science. The top nations in the world are competing in the field of science, economy and literature. This vast legacy has to be conserved and documented so that it can be bestowed to the future generation. The knowledge of this legacy is slowly getting perished in the present generation due to lack of documentation.

Keeping this in mind, the concern with retrospective acquiring of rare books has been accented recently by the burgeoning reprint industry. Maxwell Press is gratified to retrieve the rare collections with a view to bring back those books that were landmarks in their time.

In this effort, a series of rare books would be republished under the banner, "Maxwell Press". The books in the reprint series have been carefully selected for their contemporary usefulness as well as their historical importance within the intellectual. We reconstruct the book with slight enhancements made for better presentation, without affecting the contents of the original edition.

Most of the works selected for republishing covers a huge range of subjects, from history to anthropology. We believe this reprint edition will be a service to the numerous researchers and practitioners active in this fascinating field. We allow readers to experience the wonder of peering into a scholarly work of the highest order and seminal significance.

Maxwell Press

LETTER OF TRANSMITTAL.

U. S. Department of Agriculture,
Office of Experiment Stations,
Washington, D. C., May 16, 1910.

Sir: I have the honor to transmit herewith and to recommend for publication as Bulletin 227 of this Office a report of investigations on calcium, magnesium, and phosphorus in food and nutrition, carried on at Columbia University, New York City, by Henry C. Sherman, professor of organic analysis, and Arthur J. Mettler and J. Edwin Sinclair, of the department of chemistry.

The report, which supplements Professor Sherman's bulletin published by this Office on iron in food and its function in nutrition, includes a general discussion of the subject and summary of earlier literature, together with the results of six experiments on the metabolism of calcium, magnesium, and phosphorus, and a study of the amount of these mineral constituents in typical American dietaries. In general, the investigations show the importance of calcium, magnesium, and phosphorus in the diet, and the possibilities of securing these constituents by the use in proper proportion of ordinary food materials.

Respectfully,
A. C. True,
Director.

Hon. James Wilson,
Secretary of Agriculture.

CONTENTS.

CALCIUM, MAGNESIUM, AND PHOSPHORUS IN FOOD AND NUTRITION.

INTRODUCTION.

Of the elements concerned in the so-called mineral metabolism of man, at least eight—iron, calcium, magnesium, phosphorus, potassium, sodium, chlorin, and sulphur—are used in such amounts as to permit of the determination of the daily requirement by means of comparisons of intake and output.

The metabolism of iron and the iron requirements of the body have been studied and the results discussed in a previous bulletin of this series.[a] A similar investigation of each of the other elements enumerated was planned, but it has not yet been found possible to carry on the work to completion. The results which have been obtained in the preliminary study of calcium, magnesium, and phosphorus are given in this bulletin as a progress report.

OCCURRENCE AND METABOLISM OF CALCIUM AND MAGNESIUM.

There seem to be three main ways in which the so-called ash constituents may exist in the body and take part in its functions: (1) As part of the permanent structures, such as the bones; (2) as essential elements of the living substances of the active tissues; and (3) as salts held in solution in the fluids of the body and helping to give these fluids their characteristic physico-chemical properties and influence upon the elasticity and irritability of muscles and nerves. Calcium is the most abundant metallic element in the body and plays an important part in each of these three directions. Its phosphate is the chief mineral constituent of all of the bones, its combinations with proteid are essential to the highly nucleated cells which are most active in the nutritional functions, and its soluble salts have a great influence upon the properties of the body fluids and their effects upon the muscles. Magnesium is probably as widely distributed in the body as calcium, but the amount is much less, the

---

usual estimate allowing about 20 parts lime to 1 part magnesia for the body as a whole.

In general, the magnesium salts are more readily soluble in the body fluids and are not so largely deposited in the bones as are the lime salts. Thus Heiss found that of the total amounts present in the body of a dog, 99.5 per cent of the calcium and only 71 per cent of the magnesium belonged to the bones. The muscles contain more magnesia than lime, but the blood is richer in lime than in magnesia.

Of the total lime taken in the food, usually much the smaller part is excreted through the kidneys. The large proportion of ingested lime which passes out through the intestine has often been interpreted as indicating that the absorption of lime from food is poor and the calcium requirement of the body low. This inference, however, is not justified, for in the case of calcium, as also of iron, the normal path of elimination of the material broken down in the body is not through the kidneys, but through the walls of the intestines. The elimination of lime through the intestine continues even when no food is taken.

E. Voit[a] long ago demonstrated directly the elimination of lime compounds through the intestinal wall, but evidently nnderestimated the amount. According to Forster's[b] experiments, 60 per cent of the lime taken was absorbed, while only a very small portion was excreted in the urine.

The amounts of lime ordinarily excreted per day in the urine vary with the food and are given by different authors as between 0.15 and 0.5 gram.

Both the organic and the inorganic calcium compounds of the food are available to the body. While the absorption of insoluble lime salts is sometimes questioned, it has, according to Lusk,[c] been conclusively shown that such salts when eaten produce an increase in the calcium of the urine, and that, according to Rüdel,[d] blood has a special capability for carrying calcium phosphate. Lusk states that if calcium chlorid be given a little of the calcium appears in the urine and all of the chlorin. In diabetes, where a large production of acids tends to neutralize the blood, the more acid urine contains an increased amount of calcium.

According to Lusk,[c] considerations regarding the absorption of calcium apply also to magnesium. It is absorbed from the intestine in both organic and inorganic forms. If growing rabbits be fed on a

---

a Ztschr. Biol., 16 (1880), p. 55.

b Arch. Hyg., 2 (1884), p. 385.

c American Text-Book of Physiology. Philadelphia, 1900, p. 971.

d Arch. Expt. Path. u. Pharmakol., 33 (1893), p. 90.

diet poor in calcium but containing magnesium carbonate, the bones may be brought to contain double the normal quantity of magnesium, but the skeletal development remains far behind that of a normal rabbit, so that, as Weiske[a] points out, magnesium can not be considered a substitute for calcium. The magnesium salts, being more soluble than the calcium salts, occur in the urine in greater abundance. Indeed, in carnivorous animals the major part of excreted magnesium is found in the urine, the balance being given off through the intestinal wall to the feces.

It is of course especially important that the calcium and magnesium salts should be normally absorbed during the periods of infancy and childhood, when the skeleton is growing rapidly. The absence of a sufficient quantity of fat in the food (and it is thought also the presence of a greatly excessive amount) tends to deprive the growing body of its normal supply of calcium and magnesium salts, and is one of the factors in the production of nutritional disorders. The recent literature on disturbances of the calcium metabolism is far too extensive to be touched upon here.

FEEDING AND FASTING EXPERIMENTS WITH REFERENCE TO CALCIUM AND MAGNESIUM.

Several experiments have been made to show the effect of food poor in lime upon the growth and health of animals and to determine the extent to which calcium can be replaced by other alkali earths.

Weiske has given especial attention to this subject, working largely upon rabbits and using oats as the food poor in lime. The harmful effects of an exclusive oat diet have been attributed to the acidity of the products of metabolism and can be prevented at least in large measure by the addition of calcium carbonate to the food. With adults the use of magnesium carbonate seems to be equally effective. In his first experiments to determine the nutritive value of lime salts, Weiske[b] selected the sulphate and phosphate—sparingly soluble salts of rather strong acids. Five rabbits were selected for the experiment; two were killed and analyzed as controls, two fed for 47 days with oats plus calcium sulphate, and one with the same food plus calcium phosphate. Under this feeding there was no increase in weight, either of the body or of the dry, fat-free bones. The amount of mineral matter in the bones apparently decreased somewhat but not to a marked extent.

Here the sulphate and phosphate of lime evidently were not utilized by the skeleton, which was, on the other hand, apparently attacked to a slight extent by the acid products of metabolism of the

---

[a] Ztschr. Biol., 31 (1894), p. 437.

[b] Ztschr. Physiol. Chem., 20 (1895), p. 595; Jahresber. Tier-Chem., 25 (1895), p. 526.

food. Weiske believed that a more pronounced loss of mineral matter would have been shown had the feeding been continued for a longer period.

In another series of experiments Weiske found that no strontium was contained in the bones of a rabbit which had received strontium phosphate in addition to a normal diet, and that addition of calcium or magnesium phosphate to a normal diet did not increase the calcium or magnesium content of the bones above the normal.

A third experiment was made with rabbits fed on oats, a feed poor in lime but rich in the other necessary nutrients. The lime content of oats is great enough for the needs of grown animals but not for young, growing animals. Five rabbits were used. To the feed of the first no salts were added, to that of the second calcium carbonate was added daily, to that of the third calcium sulphate, to that of the fourth strontium carbonate, and to that of the fifth magnesium carbonate. The weight of the rabbits changed differently in each case. The rabbit fed without the addition of salts lost weight to a large extent. The one fed with calcium sulphate lost still more weight, and after one and a half months died after growing very lean. The animal fed with calcium carbonate gained the most weight, and the one fed with magnesium carbonate gained the next most weight. During the first month the animal fed with strontium carbonate gained as much as the one fed on magnesium carbonate; but in the last three weeks the animal lost weight. At the end of the experiment the animals were killed and the amounts of calcium, strontium, magnesium, and phosphorus were determined in the blood, the flesh, and the liver. The flesh of the rabbit fed with magnesium carbonate contained more magnesia than that of the other animals. The flesh, blood, and liver of the animal fed on strontium carbonate contained a small amount of strontia and more phosphoric acid than those of any of the other animals. Weiske concluded that with herbivora, not yet full grown and fed on a so-called acid food poor in lime, the addition of the carbonates of the alkali earths to the food so acts as to decrease or abolish the acid condition of the feed which is harmful for herbivora. The calcium carbonate gave the best results. This is evidently due to the fact that the deficiency of lime in the oats could not be compensated by magnesia or strontia, magnesium and strontium being unable to take the place of calcium in the animal economy.

The results of a lack of lime are better shown by feeding experiments of long duration in which the subject receives a sufficient amount of total food but only a small amount of calcium in any form. Under such conditions the active tissues appear to have the power of making good their losses at the expense of those parts which can be weakened with least immediate injury to the body as a whole.

Voit[a] in an experiment in which pigeons were fed with a diet poor in lime for a long time noticed no effect until the birds were killed and dissected, when it was found that although the bones concerned in locomotion were still sound, the skull and sternum were very weak and thin and in places perforated. Under similar conditions in mammals, the teeth would probably be injured also.

Weakening of the bones through lack of sufficient lime in the food is of course much more apparent during growth than in the adult. Abnormal weakness and flexibility of the bones, corresponding with rickets as observed in children, can be brought about experimentally in puppies by feeding them with meat and fat alone, while those receiving the same food with addition of bones grow normally, according to data cited by Lusk.[b]

Evidently it is not safe to assume that food furnishing sufficient protein and fuel value will necessarily furnish sufficient lime. Neither can the amount of lime excreted in the urine be taken as an indication of the lime requirements of the body. This can be ascertained only by means of metabolism experiments in which the balance of intake and output is determined.

EXPERIMENTS UPON THE INCOME AND OUTGO OF CALCIUM AND MAGNESIUM.

The purpose of this section is to bring together the results of metabolism experiments which throw light upon the calcium and magnesium requirements of healthy men, with only such data regarding diseased subjects and lower animals as appear to bear directly upon these requirements.

The earliest available work which now appears to be of value is that of Bertram,[c] who made experiments in three periods of three days each on a mixed diet of meat, fat, beer, coffee, and sodium chlorid. In period 2 he consumed in addition 40 grams of potassium citrate and in period 3, used 10 grams of calcium carbonate. His results are shown in the following table:

Daily income and outgo of lime and magnesia. Bertram's experiments.

Period.	Calcium oxid.				Magnesium oxid.			
	In food.	In urine.	In feces.	Gain (+) or loss (−).	In food.	In urine.	In feces.	Gain.
	Grams.	*Gram.*	*Grams.*	*Gram.*	*Gram.*	*Gram.*	*Gram.*	*Gram.*
First	0.385	0.167	0.233	−0.015	0.730	0.268	0.428	0.034
Second	.385	.095	.292	− .002	.730.	.269	.443	.018
Third	5.985	.298	5.414	+ .273	.730	.330	.398	.002

[a] Hermann's Handbuch der Physiologie. Leipsic, 1881, vol. 6, p. 379.
[b] American Text-Book of Physiology. Philadelphia, 1900, p. 969.
[c] Ztschr. Biol., 14 (1878), p. 354.

Gramatchikov [a] in 1890 studied five fever patients, determining in each case the income and outgo of lime and magnesia (as well as other inorganic elements) both during fever and during a period of convalescence when fever was absent. The food consisted of bread and milk, in some cases with the addition of meat, except in two cases, in which meat but no milk was taken. The figures obtained for lime are given in the tables immediately following:

Daily income and outgo of lime (CaO).   Gramatchikov's experiments.

Subject.	Period.	Body weight.	Calcium oxid.			
			In food.	In urine.	In feces.	Gain (+) or loss (−).
		Kilograms.	*Grams.*	*Gram.*	*Grams.*	*Grams.*
No. 1	Fever	55.5	2.	0.7	1,9	−0
No. 1	do	53.6	2.	.4	2 5	−
No. 1	No fever	57.6	3.	.4	1 8	+1
No. 2	Fever	58.9	3.	.1	2 7	+
No. 2	No fever	67.5	2.	.3	1 2	+
No. 3	Fever	44.0	3.	.5	2 9	+
No. 3	No fever	45.8	.	.2	2	
No. 4	Fever	53.0	4.	.4	3 6	+
No. 4	No fever	50.5	2.	.4	1 7	+
No. 5	Fever	41.0	3.	.4	2 7	
No. 5	No fever	42.3	.	.2	2	+

Daily income and outgo of magnesium oxid (MgO).   Gramatchikov's experiments.

Subject.	Period.	Body weight.	Magnesium oxid.			
			In food.	In urine.	In feces.	Gain (+) or loss (−).
		Kilograms.	*Grams.*	*Gram.*	*Gram.*	*Gram.*
No. 1	Fever	55.5	0.7	0.	0.	+0.2
No. 1	do	53.6	.8	.	.	.
No. 1	No fever	57.6	1.3	.	.	+ .
No. 2	Fever	58.9	.7	.	.	+ .
No. 2	No fever	57.5	.8	.	.	+ .
No. 3	Fever	44.0	.6	.	.	.
No. 3	No fever	45.8	.5	.	.	+ .
No. 4	Fever	53.0	.7	.	.	.
No. 4	No fever	50.5	.9	.	.	+ .
No. 5	Fever	41.0	.6	.	.	− .
No. 5	No fever	42.3	.6	.	.	.

Gramatchikov concluded that fever has little effect upon the metabolism of calcium and magnesium. If this is true the figures for these experiments should be fairly comparable with those made upon healthy subjects which follow.

The influence of adding large amounts of calcium carbonate to the food has been studied by Herxheimer [b] in metabolism experiments

a Inaug. Diss., St. Petersburg; abs. in U. S. Dept. Agr., Office Expt. Stas. Bul. 45, pp. 189, 194.

b Berlin. Klin. Wchnschr., 34 (1897), p. 423; abs. in Jahresber. Tier-Chem., 27 (1897), p. 698.

which, although arranged principally with reference to the therapeutie aspects of the practice, are interesting in showing the possibility of a large storage of calcium.

Calcium carbonate having been recommended in place of alkali carbonate for the treatment of uric acid concretions of the kidneys and used in the shape of "lime bread," the action of this bread was studied by Herxheimer in an eleven-day experiment. After three normal days an average of 300 grams of bread containing 18 grams calcium carbonate were given per day on the next five days, and for the next three days an average of 300 grams of "2 per cent bread" containing 6 grams of calcium carbonate were given. The results were as follows:

The volume of urine, the nitrogen balance, and the excretion of uric acid were not influenced by the supply of lime to any noticeable degree. Most of the lime excreted was given out in the feces and only a small part in the urine. Not less than 15.9 grams of the supplied lime remained, however, in the body. The total phosphoric acid excreted remained practically the same during the whole experiment; the phosphate in the urine decreased, while that in the feces increased correspondingly. The monosodium phosphate in the urine decreased, while the disodium phosphate increased. The acidity of the urine proportionally decreased and attained a weakly acid or amphoteric state.

Gottstein[a] determined the income and outgo of calcium and magnesium in metabolism experiments in which casein and edestin were fed either with or without the addition of mixtures of salts. As the experiments all gave a negative balance for calcium and magnesium, the influence of the different proteid bodies on the matabolism of the alkali earths could not be positively determined. The excretion of magnesium increased with that of nitrogen. In nitrogen storage the magnesium loss was less. In these experiments calcium showed no such relation. Phosphorus and magnesium balances changed in like manner, but no relation of calcium to phosphorus could be discovered. The reported parallelism of the phosphorus and magnesium balances in this experiment is interesting, as Loew has found that the metabolism of these two elements in plants is closely connected, magnesium apparently serving as a phosphate carrier in vegetable metabolism.

Renvall's[b] investigations were made primarily to determine the need of adult man for phosphorus, calcium, and magnesium. The subject (Renvall) was 22 years old, 174 centimeters high, and weighed 71.1 kilograms. He was of a nervous temperament and

---

[a] Inaug. Diss., Breslau, 1901; abs. in Jahresber. Tier-Chem., 31 (1901), p. 636.

[b] Skand. Arch. Physiol., 16 (1904), p. 94.

worked about 15 hours daily in the laboratory, sleeping 7 hours. Renvall says of his physical condition, "sehr reichlichte Salzsäureabsonderung im Ventrikel sonst völlig gesund."

The experiment lasted 32 days, and the diet consisted of dry bread, smoked ham, cheese, butter, oatmeal, zwieback, sodium chlorid, and in the last 17 days of the experiment, chalk.

The experiment was divided into five periods of 8, 7, 6, 5, and 5 days, respectively. Nothing was eaten for 18 hours before and after the experiment, and the separation of the feces was accomplished by eating dried blueberries for markers.

Calcium and magnesium were determined in the urine by precipitating with ammonium hydroxid, filtering and dissolving the precipitate in dilute hydrochloric acid, and then adding ammonium acetate and a few drops of glacial acetic acid. Ammonium oxalate in solution was then added to the hot solution to precipitate the calcium. After standing 6 hours the calcium oxalate was filtered off and ignited and weighed as CaO. In the filtrate the magnesium was precipitated with ammonium hydroxid, filtered, ignited, and weighed as $Mg_2P_2O_7$. For each determination 200 cubic centimeters of urine were taken.

Calcium and magnesium in the feces were found by ashing, dissolving the ash in hydrochloric acid, and precipitating the phosphorus with ammonium acetate and ferric chlorid, and reprecipitating twice. In the filtrate, after boiling to small bulk, the lime was precipitated as oxalate, and in this filtrate the magnesium was precipitated as magnesium ammonium phosphate with ammonium hydroxid and sodium phosphate.

The nitrogen balance was as follows:

Daily income and outgo of nitrogen. Renvall's experiments.

Period.	Nitrogen.			
	In food.	In urine.	In feces.	Gain (+) or loss (−).
	Grams.	Grams.	Grams.	Grams.
First	12.10	15.29	2.15	−5.34
Second	13.70	14.02	2.34	−2.66
Third	16.10	16.28	2.56	−2.74
Fourth	22.73	19.64	2.95	+ .14
Fifth	21.22	20.10	3.59	−2.47

The calcium balance is given below:

Daily income and outgo of calcium (Ca).   Renvall's experiments.

Period.	Calcium.			
	In food.	In urine.	In feces.	Gain (+) or loss (−).
	Grams.	*Gram.*	*Grams.*	*Gram.*
First	0.860	0.507	0.325	+0.028
Second	.909	.595	.331	− .017
Third	1.197	.557	.476	+ .164
Fourth	1.486	.649	.664	+ .173
Fifth	1.470	.609	.850	+ .011
Eight days following first period	....	.505	1.230	....
Six days following second period	....	.374	.661	....
Eight days following third period	....	.401	1.178	....

The chief peculiarity here is the large amount of calcium in the urine. In the first three periods the amount of lime in the urine is greater than that in the feces, while in other experiments (Bertram, Herxheimer, etc.) the opposite is the rule. In the first period there was almost a calcium equilibrium. From the increased storage of lime in the third and fourth periods, in which calcium carbonate was added to the food, it is seen that the body absorbed lime from the calcium carbonate given. In the last period, however, there apparently occurred no absorption of lime from the calcium carbonate. The results obtained indicate that the body tends toward a calcium equilibrium, which would account for the rapid falling off in the storage of lime in the fifth period.

· From the first period it is seen that the body can maintain calcium equilibrium with less than 0.860 gram Ca per day. In Bertram's experiment the subject apparently showed calcium equilibrium with about 0.400 gram CaO.

The magnesium balance is given below:

Daily income and outgo of magnesium (Mg).   Renvall's experiments.

Period.	Magnesium.			
	In food.	In urine.	In feces.	Gain (+) or loss (−).
	Gram.	*Gram.*	*Gram.*	*Gram.*
First	0.412	0.139	0.286	−0.013
Second	.499	.132	.326	+ .041
Third	.559	.143	.337	+ .079
Fourth	.621	.170	.327	+ .124
Fifth	.625	.171	.398	+ .056
Eight days following first period	....	.142	.242	....
Six days following second pe	....	.147	.258	....
Eight days following third period	....	.149	.263	....

Renvall also studied the source of nitrogen, phosphorus, calcium, and magnesium eliminated by the intestine. It is known that the feces contain substances which are not the residue of the food eaten, but are products of the body, either excretory products or residues of the digestive juices not absorbed. The excretory products can be best studied in feces from fasting subjects. The feces in starvation, however, can not be compared to normal feces, as the latter contain not only the excretion products contained in the former, but also substances given off in the process of digestion, and it is probable that these are in larger quantities as the food eaten increases. It is as yet impossible to differentiate between the above products, but an idea as to the amount of these different substances can be obtained by examining the feces from a diet very poor in the element or substance under investigation. Renvall made experiments in this way on himself and two friends. He used a diet poor in nitrogen, phosphorus, calcium, and magnesium (sago, water, and sugar), and the feces were separated by using blueberries as a marker after 18 hours' fasting. The calcium balance is given below, while the magnesium balance is given in the table immediately following it:

Daily income and outgo of calcium (Ca). Renvall's experiments.

Subject.	Duration of test.	Calcium oxid.			
		In food.	In urine.	In feces.	Loss.
		Gram.	*Gram.*	*Gram.*	*Gram.*
Renvall	First day	0.101	0.176	0.165	0.240
Do	Second day	.079	.118	.165	.204
Subject No. 1	First day	.116	.044	.163	.091
Do	Second day	.126	.045	.163	.082
Subject No. 2	First day	.070	.060	....	....
Do	Second day	.061	.044	....	....

Daily income and outgo of magnesium (Mg). Renvall's experiments.

Subject.	Duration of test.	Magnesium.			
		In food.	In urine.	In feces.	Loss.
		Gram.	*Gram.*	*Gram.*	*Gram.*
Renvall	First day	0.026	0.074	0.067	0.115
Renvall	Second day	.021	.065	.067	.111
Subject No. 1	First day	.030	....	.064	....
Subject No. 1	Second day	.032	.029	.064	.061
Subject No. 2	First day	.019	.045	....	....
Subject No. 2	Second day	.016	.038	....	....

Von Wendt,[a] following methods somewhat similar to those of Renvall, with whose work he appears to have been intimately acquainted, has determined the income and outgo of calcium and magnesium (as well as of nitrogen, iron, phosphorus, sulphur, and chlorin) in an extended series of experiments, partly with food poor both in ash constituents and in protein, partly with a diet containing ample protein but insufficient ash constituents. In many cases, also, known amounts of pure salts were taken with the food; and finally the series was concluded with a metabolism experiment in which the subject took the kinds and amounts of food to which he had been accustomed in ordinary life. A diet of the first description consisting of sago, sugar, and butter was taken during experiments Nos. 1, 2, 3, and 4; one of the second sort consisting of bread, butter, sugar, and coagulated white of egg was taken in experiment No. 5, periods A and B; and one of the third sort consisting of bread, butter, meat, cheese, tea, and sugar, was taken in experiment No. 6.

The separation of the feces was accomplished by giving 2 grams of carbon (lampblack) at the first or last mealtime of each experiment.

From the diet of sago, butter, and sugar Von Wendt obtained 0.10–0.15 gram phosphorus, about 0.04 gram calcium, and 0.015 gram magnesium. The feces from this diet contained the smallest amounts of phosphorus, calcium, and magnesium yet noted in any except fasting experiments, viz, 0.099 gram phosphorus, 0.156 gram calcium, and 0.015 gram magnesium. The feces, therefore, contained practically the same amount of phosphorus and magnesium, and four times as much calcium as was taken in the food. Here at least 0.106 gram of calcium from the body was excreted through the intestine, and this, if excreted in the form of phosphate, would account for all the phosphorus which the feces contained. The amount of magnesium is only a trifle larger than was found by Müller in the fasting feces of Cetti and Breithaupt, indicating that the digestion and absorption of enough carbohydrates and fats to yield 1,500 to 3,000 calories per day does not appreciably increase the intestinal elimination of magnesium.

According to Von Wendt, the capacity of the urine for dissolving calcium salts does not regulate the amount excreted by the urine. In the acid urine the calcium is in a soluble form, while in the alkaline feces the calcium is present mostly in insoluble forms, probably as tricalcium phosphate. Calcium is transferred from the blood into the intestines probably as dicalcium and monocalcium phosphate. As only the monocalcium phosphate is soluble in the weakly alkaline intestinal secretions, Von Wendt believes that calcium is probably mostly absorbed in this form. He calls attention to the fact that the

---

[a] Skand. Arch. Physiol., 17 (1905), p. 211.

proportion of calcium absorbed to phosphorus absorbed is about the same as that of calcium to phosphorus in monocalcium phosphate, the slight difference being accounted for by the fact that dicalcium phosphate is also slightly soluble in the intestinal juices. This reasoning is, however, open to the objection that there is as yet no accurate measure of the calcium absorbed, the unabsorbed calcium and that which has been used in the body and excreted through the intestinal wall appearing together in the feces.

Von Wendt found that the consumption of common salt increases the renal and decreases the intestinal elimination of calcium. In experiment No. 6 on ordinary mixed diet practically uniform, both qualitatively and quantitatively, two subjects gave the following results:

With Subject G the daily excretion of calcium in the urine was 0.22 gram and in the feces 0.85 gram, making a total of 1.07 grams.

With Subject L the quantity excreted in the urine was 0.09 gram and in the feces 1 gram, making a total of 1.09 grams.

This difference was found by further trials to be due to the fact that Subject G took more salt on his food than Subject L, and Von Wendt states that the greater the amount of sodium chlorid consumed the greater the renal elimination and the smaller the intestinal elimination of calcium.

Von Wendt discusses at length the probable forms of phosphate eliminated in the feces and in the urine, and seems to believe that the relative abundance of phosphorus and of bases will govern the proportions of acid, neutral, and tribasic phosphates, and thus determine the proportion of phosphorus eliminated through the intestine.

Results of Von Wendt's experiments follow in tabular form.

227

Income and outgo of calcium oxid (CaO).   Von Wendt's experiments.

Experiment.	Food and supplements.	Calcium oxid.			
		In food.	In urine.	In feces.	Gain (+) or loss (−).
Experiment No. 1:		*Grams.*	*Gram.*	*Grams.*	*Gram.*
First day	Sago, sugar, and butter	0.035	0.040	0.156	−0.161
Second day	do	.050	.020	.156	− .126
Third day	Sago, sugar, and butter, with 0.1 gram Fe as carbonate.	.044	.100	(.156)	(− .122)
Fourth day	Sago, sugar, and butter, with 2 grams $CaSO_4$ and 0.09 gram Fe .	.053	....	(.156)	....
Experiment No. 2:					
First day	Sago, sugar, and butter	.024	.036	.240	− .252
Second day	do	.037	.020	.240	− .223
Third day	Sago, sugar, and butter, with 4 grams NaCl.	.035	.022	.240	− .227
Experiment No. 3:					
First day	Sago, sugar, and butter, with 5 grams NaCl and 3 grams $CaHPO_4$.	.920	.059	.479	+ .382
Second day	Sago, sugar, and butter, with 8 grams NaCl and 3 grams $CaHPO_4$.	.920	.081	.510	+ .329
Third day	Sago, sugar, and butter, with 12 grams NaCl and 3 grams $CaHPO_4$.	.922	.066	.549	+ .307
Experiment No. 4:					
First day	Sago, sugar, and butter, with 5 grams NaCl and 3 grams $CaHPO_4$.	.916	.127	.413	+ .376
Second day	do	.917	.114	.413	+ .390
Experiment No. 5:					
Period A—					
First day	Bread, butter, sugar, and egg white	.283	.111	.310	− .138
Second day	do	.273	.115	.805	− .647
Third day	do	.266	.100	.962	− .796
Fourth day	Bread, butter, sugar, and egg white, with 3 grams $CaHPO_4$.	1.145	.133	.400	+ .612
Fifth day	Bread, butter, sugar, and egg white	.262	.154	.400	− .292
Sixth day	Bread, butter, sugar, and egg white, with 10 grams NaCl.	.261	.137	.256	− .132
Seventh day	Bread, butter, sugar, and egg white, with 20 grams NaCl.	.262	.206	.256	− .200
Period B—					
First day	Bread, butter, sugar, and egg white	.161	.151	.256	− .246
Second day	Bread, butter, sugar, and egg white, with 3 grams ammonium citrate.	.171	.131	.242	− .202
Third day	Bread, butter, sugar, and egg white, with 0.038 gram Fe (sulph. ferr.).	.173	.104	.254	− .185
Fourth day	Bread, butter, sugar, and egg white, with 1 gram K_2CO_3.	.157	.083	.254	− .180
Fifth day	Bread, butter, sugar, and egg white, with 2.25 grams ammonium citrate and 2.25 grams $CaHPO_4$.	.820	.079	.640	+ .101
Sixth day	Bread, butter, sugar, and egg white, with 3 grams ammonium citrate and 3 grams $CaHPO_4$.	1.049	.078	.894	+ .077
Seventh day	Bread, butter, sugar, and egg white	.070	.078	.340	− .348
Period C—					
First day	Bread, butter, sugar, and meat, with 3 grams NaCl.	.223	.124	.310	− .211
Second day	Bread, butter, sugar, and meat	.177	.209	.310	− .342
Experiment No. 6:					
Period G—					
First day	Bread, butter, meat, cheese, tea, and sugar, with 2 grams NaCl.	1.063	.165	1.001	− .103
Second day	Bread, butter, meat, cheese, tea, and sugar, with 8 grams NaCl.	1.230	.226	1.001	+ .003
Third day	Bread, butter, meat, cheese, tea, and sugar, with 15 grams NaCl.	1.230	.277	1.001	− .048
Fourth day	Bread, butter, meat, cheese, tea, and sugar, with 15.5 grams NaCl.	1.230	.318	1.824	− .912
Period L—					
First day	Bread, butter, meat, cheese, tea, and sugar, with 2 grams NaCl.	1.063	.132	1.005	− .074
Second day	Bread, butter, meat, cheese, tea, and sugar, with 8 grams NaCl.	1.230	.173	1.005	+ .052
Third day	Bread, butter, meat, cheese, tea, and sugar.	1.230	.189	1.005	+ .036

Income and outgo of magnesium oxid (MgO).   Von Wendt's experiments.

Experiment.	Food and supplements.	Magnesium oxid.			
		In food.	In urine.	In fœces.	Gain (+) or loss (−).
Experiment No. 1:		*Gram.*	*Gram.*	*Gram.*	*Gram.*
First day..........	Sago, sugar, and butter.................	0.011	0.044	0.015	−0.048
Second day........	....do.................................	.016	.033	.015	− .032
Third day.........	Sago, sugar, and butter, with 0.1 gram Fe as carbonate.	.014	.030	(.015)	(− .031)
Fourth day........	Sago, sugar, and butter, with 2 grams CaSO₄ and 0.09 gram Fe.	.017	.026	(.015)	(− .024)
Experiment No. 2:					
First day..........	a o, sugar, and butter....................	.008	.020	.040	− .052
Second day........	S. g do.................................	.012	.028	.040	− .056
Third day.........	Sago, sugar, and butter, with 4 grams NaCl..	.012	.029	.040	− .057
Experiment No. 3:					
First day..........	Sago, sugar, and butter, with 5 grams NaCl and 3 grams CaHPO₄.	.012	.036	.019	− .043
Second day........	Sago, sugar, and butter, with 8 grams NaCl and 3 grams CaHPO₄.	.014	.032	.020	− .038
Third day.........	Sago, sugar, and butter, with 12 grams NaCl and 3 grams CaHPO₄.	.013	.069	.022	− .078
Experiment No. 4:					
First day..........	Sago, sugar, and butter, with 5 grams NaCl and 3 grams CaHPO₄.	.012	.049	.028	− .065
Second day........	.....do..................................	.011	.045	.028	− .062
Experiment No. 5:					
Period A—					
First day......	Bread, butter, sugar, and egg white........	.224	.058	.174	− .008
Second day....	....do.................................	.212	.068	.137	+ .007
Third day......	....do.................................	.204	.086	.098	+ .020
Fourth day....	Bread, butter, sugar, and egg white, with 3 grams CaHPO₄.	.205	.103	.092	+ .010
Fifth day......	Bread, butter, sugar, and egg white........	.202	.086	.092	+ .024
Sixth day......	Bread, butter, sugar, and egg white, with 10 grams NaCl.	.201	.092	.099	+ .010
Seventh day...	Bread, butter, sugar, and egg white, with 20 grams NaCl.	.202	.110	.099	− .007
Period B—					
First day......	Bread, butter, sugar, and egg white........	.078	.084	.099	− .105
Second day....	Bread, butter, sugar, and egg white, with 3 grams ammonium citrate.	.078	.076	.078	− .076
Third day.....	Bread, butter, sugar, and egg white, with 0.038 gram Fe (sulph. ferr.).	.079	.061	.050	− .032
Fourth day....	Bread, butter, sugar, and egg white, with 1 gram K₂CO₃.	.070	.057	.076	− .063
Fifth day......	Bread, butter, sugar, and egg white, with 2.25 grams ammonium citrate and 2.25 grams CaHPO₄.	.073	.049	.060	− .036
Sixth day......	Bread, butter, sugar, and egg white, with 3 grams ammonium citrate and 3 grams CaHPO₄.	.078	.031	.040	+ .007
Seventh day...	Bread, butter, sugar, and egg white........	.018	.034	.030	− .046
Period C—					
First day......	Bread, butter, sugar, and meat, with 3 grams NaCl.	.260	.021	.213	+ .026
Second day....	Bread, butter, sugar, and meat.............	.211	.028	.213	− .030
Experiment No. 6:					
Period G—					
First day......	Bread, butter, meat, cheese, tea, and sugar, with 2 grams NaCl.	.320	.085	.242	− .007
Second day....	Bread, butter, meat, cheese, tea, and sugar, with 8 grams NaCl.	.327	.125	.242	− .040
Third day.....	Bread, butter, meat, cheese, tea, and sugar, with 15 grams NaCl.	.327	.129	.242	− .044
Fourth day....	Bread, butter, meat, cheese, tea, and sugar, with 15.5 grams NaCl.	.327	.123	.192	+ .012
Period L—					
First day......	Bread, butter, meat, cheese, tea, and sugar, with 2 grams NaCl.	.320	.103	.234	− .017
Second day....	Bread, butter, meat, cheese, tea, and sugar, with 8 grams NaCl.	.327	.119	.234	− .026
Third day.....	Bread, butter, meat, cheese, tea, and sugar..	.327	.122	.234	− .029

OCCURRENCE AND METABOLISM OF PHOSPHORUS.

Phosphorus, like calcium, is an important constituent of the bones, of the active tissues, and also of the body fluids. Calcium phosphate is the chief mineral ingredient of bone and is supposed to constitute about three-fourths of the entire ash of the body. Phosphorus compounds are also the most prominent as constituents of the muscles and blood corpuscles and stand next to the chlorids in abundance in the plasma and lymph. Voit estimated that a human body weighing 70 kilograms (154 pounds) would contain: In the bones, 1,400 grams phosphorus; in the muscles, 130 grams; in the brain and nerves, 12 grams.

As the phosphorus of the tissues exists largely in the form of nucleo-proteids and nucleins—the characteristic substances of cell nuclei—and as these cell constituents are most active in metabolism, whereas the material of the bones is commonly assumed to be comparatively inactive, there has been a tendency to regard the phosphorus metabolism as in some degree a measure of the nucleo-proteid metabolism, as the output of nitrogen is taken as a measure of the metabolism of protein in general.

Several investigators[a] have studied the urinary excretion of phosphates as influenced by those conditions which are believed to be connected with the metabolism of nucleins, and an intimate connection between changes in the phosphorus eliminated and in the katabolism of nucleins is evidently assumed by Dunlop, Paton, Stockmann, and Maccadam[b] in interpreting the results of their investigations of the effect of muscular exertion. In these experiments each subject was kept on a uniform diet for 7 days, on the fourth of which as much exercise (bicycle riding) was taken as could be endured without serious discomfort. In each case the day or days following the exertion showed an increased elimination of nitrogen and sulphur, but only when the subject was in poor training was there a corresponding increase in the elimination of phosphates and of uric acid. From this it was concluded that with the subject in good training only simple proteid is broken down, while if the subject be in poor training this consumption of simple proteid is accompanied by a consumption of nucleo-proteid. In this connection it is interesting to note the observation previously made by Preysz,[c]

---

[a] Moraczewski. Arch. Path. Anat. u. Physiol. [Virchow], 151 (1898), p. 22; Milroy and Malcom. Jour. Physiol., 23 (1898), p. 217, and 25 (1899), p. 105; White and Hopkins, Ibid., 24 (1899), p. 42; Loewi. Arch. Expt. Path. u. Pharmakol., 44 (1900–1), p. 1; abs. in Jour. Chem. Soc. [London], 78 (1900), II, p. 417.

[b] Jour. Physiol., 22 (1897–98), p. 68.

[c] Ungar. Arch. Med., 1 (1892–93), p. 38; rev. in Arch. Physiol. [Pflüger], 54 (1893), p. 21.

that the increased elimination of phosphoric acid resulting from walking a given distance (25 kilometers) was considerably greater when the distance was walked at a rapid rate, causing a more intense though less prolonged exertion.

On the other hand, it was early shown by Voit that the body material katabolized during fasting comes quite largely from the bones; and Jordan, Hart, and Patten,[a] as the result of an extended investigation of the phosphorus compounds of feeding stuffs and their behavior when fed to herbivorous animals, have concluded that the phosphorus metabolism consists largely in the formation of inorganic phosphates from comparatively simple organic compounds such as phytin.

Whether the phosphorus elimination can in any case be taken as an indication of nucleo-proteid metabolism or not, it is certain that the output of phosphorus and the output of nitrogen do not run parallel and can not, therefore, be measures of the same set of metabolic changes.

In a set of experiments by Sherman and Hawk,[b] carried out primarily for the purpose of studying the time relations of the elimination of nitrogen, sulphur, and phosphorus after ingestion of meat, the course of renal elimination of these three elements was observed simultaneously, the urine being collected in 3-hour periods during the day with a 9-hour period at night. The rates of elimination for nitrogen and sulphur were found to run nearly parallel, rising and falling twice during the day and reaching a minimum during the night. The fluctuations, though quite regular, were not very great, the highest rate of elimination found for any 3-hour period during the day being usually only about one-fourth greater than the average rate for the 9 hours of the night. On the other hand, in the elimination of phosphorus the fluctuations, though less regular, were considerably larger, the maximum rate of elimination being two or three times the minimum. The minimum rate of elimination of phosphorus, unlike that of nitrogen and sulphur, was reached not during the night but at some time in the forenoon, usually from 1 to 3 hours, but sometimes from 4 to 6 hours, after rising. Moreover, these experiments taken in connection with those of Rosemann[c] and Roeske[d] appear to indicate that the output of phosphorus is more affected by sleep and other factors of the daily routine and less affected by food than is the elimination of nitrogen and sulphur.

---

[a] New York State Sta. Tech. Bul. 1; Amer. Jour. Physiol., 16 (1906), p. 268.

[b] Amer. Jour. Physiol., 4 (1900), p. 25; 10 (1903), p. 115; 10 (1904), p. 269.

[c] Arch. Physiol. [Pflüger], 65 (1897), p. 343.

[d] Ueber den Verlauf der Phosphorsaure-Ausscheidung beim Menschen. Inaug. Diss., Griefswald, 1897.

While the nitrogen and phosphorus metabolism are thus largely independent in their general course, it is essential for the growth of new tissue that phosphorus shall be stored as well as nitrogen. Hence, when there is a storage of nitrogen sufficiently prolonged to represent tissue growth, it would seem probable that a parallel storage of phosphorus would occur. In most cases which have been studied, a prolonged gain of nitrogen has been found to be accompanied by a gain of phosphorus, and vice versa, but among adults there are many exceptions to this rule, as for example when the food is comparatively rich in phosphorus and poor in nitrogen. Under such conditions very pronounced loss of body nitrogen may be accompanied by equilibrium or even by gain of phosphorus.

The importance of phosphorus as building material for the growing organism is strikingly indicated by the way in which nature provides a milk richer in phosphorus in those species in which the growth of the young is proportionally rapid as shown by the following table based mainly upon the work of Bunge[a] and his pupils.

Relation of milk to rate of growth, in man and animals.

Species.	Time required for new-born to double the birth weight.	Proportion of principal building material in the milk.		
		Protein.	Calcium oxid.	Phosphorus pentoxid.
	Days.	*Per cent.*	*Per cent.*	*Per cent.*
Man	180	1.6	0.03	0.05
Horse	60	2.0	.12	.13
Cow	47	3.5	.16	.20
Goat	22	3.7	.20	.28
Sheep	15	4.9	.25	.29
Swine	14	5.2	.25	.31
Dog	9	7.4	.45	.51
Rabbit	6	14.4	.89	.99

TYPES OF PHOSPHOROUS COMPOUNDS IN FOODS AND THEIR NUTRITIVE RELATIONS.

The most abundant of the phosphorous compounds of food thus far studied may be grouped provisionally under four heads: (1) Inorganic phosphates; (2) simple organic derivatives of phosphoric acid and phosphates (phytin, etc.); (3) phosphorized fats (lecithin, etc.); and (4) phosphorized proteids (nucleo-proteids, nucleo-albumins).

Miescher[b] studied the formation of complex from simpler phosphorous compounds in the animal body by observations upon the Rhine salmon. During the breeding season these fish remain a long time in fresh water, taking no food but developing large masses of

[a] Abderhalden's Physiologische Chemie. Berlin, 1906, p. 433.
[b] Arch. Exp. Path. Pharm., 37 (1896), p. 100.

roe and milt at the expense of molecular tissue. This process appears to involve the formation of considerable amounts of phosphorized proteids and fats, from simple proteids and fats and inorganic phosphates. The conclusions reached by Miescher have in the main been confirmed by the recent investigations of Paton[a] in Scotland.

Maxwell[b] investigated the relations of lecithin and phosphates with reference to both plant and animal metabolism. The plant ordinarily receives its phosphorus almost entirely in the form of inorganic phosphates from which it builds up representatives of all of the above-mentioned groups of organic phosphorous compounds. At the time of Maxwell's investigations the wide distribution of notable amounts of phytin compounds was not recognized and it is probable that the phosphorus occurring in this form (especially in seeds) was considered by Maxwell as belonging to the mineral phosphates. Maxwell found in germinating seeds an increase of lecithin at the expense of phosphates [and phytin].

A similar formation of lecithin from phosphates appeared to take place in eggs during the first stages of incubation, from which it would appear that not only in the fully developed animal (as observed by Miescher) but also in the earliest metabolic activities within the egg, it is possible for animal cells to synthesize lecithins from simpler phosphorous compounds. In the later stages of incubation, as the bones of the chick developed, there was a marked decrease of lecithins and increase of phosphates, indicating that lecithin is largely concerned in the growth of even such tissues as bone.

Chiefly on account of certain peculiarities which had been observed in the artificial digestion of casein, the digestibility and nutritive value of the phosphorized radicles of phospho-proteid was for some time in doubt. In 1897, however, Marcuse,[c] working in Rohmann's laboratory, showed by a series of digestion and metabolism experiments with dogs that about 90 per cent of the phosphorus of the casein fed was absorbed and apparently well utilized.

Steinitz,[d] in continuing the work begun by Marcuse, studied especially the question whether the phospho-proteids when fed to the exclusion of phosphates were able to support a storage of phosphorus in the body. In these experiments, dogs were fed with casein (in the form of nutrose) or with ovovitellin, with the addition in each case of cane sugar and a mixture of salts containing sodium, potassium, and calcium chlorid, magnesium citrate, and iron citrate. In a control experiment the food consisted of myosin, rice starch,

---

[a] Jour. Physiol., 22 (1898), p. 333.

[b] Amer. Chem. Jour., 13 (1891), p. 16; 15 (1893), p. 185.

[c] Arch. Physiol. [Pflüger], 67 (1897), p. 373.

[d] Ibid., 72 (1898), p. 75.

bacon, meat extract, and meat ash with distilled water. In these experiments the phospho-proteids gave better results in the storage of phosphorus than did the control diet containing mainly simple proteids and inorganic phosphates.

Zadik[a] and Leipziger,[b] apparently working independently, though both in Rohmann's laboratory, supplemented the work of Steinitz by similar metabolism experiments in which edestin was fed. Both found that here also the phosphorus balance was distinctly less favorable upon a mixture of phosphates and simple proteids than on a diet containing phosphorized proteids in corresponding amounts.

Rohmann,[c] in summarizing and discussing the work thus carried out in his laboratory, and especially the experiments of Steinitz and Leipziger, compares the results as follows:

Calculated daily storage of phosphorus on different diets.

Characteristic food of period.	Phosphorus resorbed per kilogram body weight.	Phosphorus stored per kilogram body weight.
	Gram.	*Milligrams.*
Nutrose (casein preparation)	0. 0343	8. 8
Vitellin (from egg yolk)	. 0283	20. 9
Myosin (with phosphates)	. 055	. 1
Edestin (with phosphates)	. 051	. 1

It should be noted in connection with this method of stating the difference between the results on the two types of diet that in the experiments with the phosphorized proteids (especially in the case of vitellin) the amounts of phosphorus eliminated by the intestine were larger than with myosin and edestin and it is not improbable that at least a part of this fecal phosphorus may have been utilized by the body and then eliminated through the intestinal wall instead of through the kidneys. After making full allowance for this possibility, however, there remains a very striking difference in the phosphorus balance in favor of the phosphorized proteids as opposed to the mixtures of simple proteids with inorganic phosphates.

The storage of nitrogen was also more pronounced in the periods in which the phosphorized proteids were fed. Rohmann concludes that the nutritive functions of phosphorized and phosphorus-free proteids are not the same, the former being especially adapted to furnish the material for tissue growth.

---

a. Arch. Physiol. [Pflüger], 77 (1899), p. 1.
b Ibid., 78 (1899), p. 402.
c Berlin. Klin. Wchnschr., 35 (1898), p. 789.

In this connection it is interesting to note that when casein is digested with trypsin, about two-thirds of the phosphorus remains in organic combination.[a]

Ehrström[b] experimented upon himself to determine the effect of replacing a known amount of organic food phosphorus by mineral phosphate. The organic phosphorus was taken mainly in the form of "proton," a casein preparation which was taken in bread in order to make it more palatable. The phosphorus balance was determined during three periods: (1) On freely chosen food; (2) on a diet of 1 liter milk and 500 grams proton bread; and (3) on a diet of 1 liter milk and 500 grams wheat bread and $CaHPO_4$ somewhat more than sufficient to replace the phosphorus of the proton. The result was as follows:

Daily income and outgo of nitrogen and phosphorus, as affected by substituting mineral phosphates for food phosphates. Ehrström's experiments.

Character of diet.	Dura-tion of period.	In food.	In urine and feces.	Gain (+) or loss (−).
	Days.	*Grams.*	*Grams.*	*Grams.*
Ordinary food:				
Nitrogen	7	17.29	18.60	−1.31
Phosphorus	7	2.48	1.87	+ .01
Milk and proton bread:				
Nitrogen	6	17.85	17.27	+ .58
Phosphorus	6	2.09	1.45	+ .44
Milk and wheat bread, with $CaHPO_4$:				
Nitrogen	5	12.55	14.36	−1.81
Phosphorus	5	2.27	2.04	+ .23

Comparison of the second and third periods shows that in the latter the amount of phosphorus stored was considerably decreased, although the amount fed was increased. The interpretation of the results is somewhat complicated by the fact that the amount of phosphorus in the feces was greater in the third period than in the first; but even if it be assumed that only the phosphorus of the food minus that of the feces was available to the body the difference in the phosphorus balance is still sufficiently large to indicate that the phosphorus in the form of phospho-proteid was of distinctly greater nutritive value than that in the form of phosphate.

A further confirmation of this fact is found in the work of Gumpert,[c] who, in an experiment upon a man, found that 1.88 grams of phosphoric anhydrid given mainly in the form of casein kept the subject in practical equilibrium, whereas the substitution of meat for the casein, while decreasing the amount of phosphoric anhydrid in the

---

[a] Bayliss and Plimmer in Cohen's Organic Chemistry. p. 430; Jour. Physiol., 33 (1906), p. 439.

[b] Skand. Arch. Physiol., 14 (1903), p. 82.

[c] Med. Klinik., 1 (1905), p. 1037.

food by only 0.08 gram, caused a loss of 0.25 to 0.40 gram from the body, a result which is evidently due to the fact that the phosphorus of the casein was of greater nutritive value than that of the meat, about half of the latter being in the form of phosphates.

It does not follow, however, that the phosphorus of phosphates is without nutritive value, nor even as concluded by Zadik,[a] that the body is incapable of utilizing it for tissue growth. Keller,[b] in a study of the phosphorus metabolism of young children, found evidence that storage of phosphorus was favored by food which contained a liberal supply of phosphates in addition to phospho-proteids and phosphorized fats. Ehrström, also, in the discussion of his results above quoted, assigns to the inorganic phosphates a distinct value in nutrition, and from the data of a recent investigation by Von Wendt[c] it may be seen that the loss of phosphorus occurring on a diet poor in ash was greatly reduced when dicalcium phosphate was added to the ration without any change in the food consumed. The inorganic phosphates appear also to have a prominent part in maintaining the proper degree of neutrality in the body fluids, as shown by Henderson and his associates.[d]

Active investigations regarding the nutritive values of the phytin compounds and of the phosphorized fats being now in progress, any attempt to summarize the knowledge on these points would be premature at this time.

In general it appears that all four types of phosphorus compounds are utilized in nutrition, but that considerable differences in nutritive value probably exist.

It is doubtless largely for this reason that experiments upon the intake and output of phosphorus have given such variable indications as to the amount required for the maintenance of equilibrium in man. One subject has shown equilibrium on a diet furnishing 0.82 gram phosphorus (equivalent to 1.88 grams P_2O_5) per day, and another has lost phosphorus while on a diet which furnished 2.07 grams (equivalent to 4.74 grams of P_2O_5) per day. Probably also the phosphorus output like the nitrogen output is governed to some extent by the previous habit of the organism, so that the balance of intake and output for a short period may not show the actual phosphorus requirement, but something between this and the amount ordinarily eaten.

[a] Arch. Physiol. [Pflüger], 77 (1899), p. 1.

[b] Arch. Kinderheilk., 29 (1900), p. 1.

[c] Skand. Arch. Physiol., 17 (1905), p. 211.

[d] Amer. Jour. Physiol., 15 (1906), p. 257; 18 (1907), pp. 113, 250; Jour. Med. Research, 16 (1907), p. 1; Abs. in Chem. Abst., 1 (1907), pp. 1020, 1292.

Without attempting any discussion of individual experiments upon the phosphorus requirement (satisfactory interpretation of which must await further knowledge of the distribution and relative amounts of the different types of phosphorus compounds in foods), the general bearing of such experiments will be considered after the metabolism experiments of the present investigation have been described.

METABOLISM EXPERIMENTS OF THE PRESENT INVESTIGATION.

The present investigation included 6 metabolism experiments, each of three days' duration, in which the balance of intake and output was determined for calcium, magnesium, and phosphorus. In three of the experiments the metabolism of iron was also studied, and the experimental conditions have been fully described and the iron balances discussed in a previous publication.[a] Such general details of these three experiments as are essential to the reporting of the studies of calcium and magnesium are summarized in the present publication. In all six experiments the subject was the same—a healthy man engaged in laboratory work. The diet of each experiment was decided upon in advance and was identical for each of the three days of each experiment.

Each experimental day began at 7 a. m. and the food was taken in three nearly equal meals, at 7.30 a. m., and 12.20 and 6.30 p. m. The urine of each experimental day was mixed, weighed, and sampled for analysis and for the preparation of a composite sample representing the entire experiment. The feces for each 3-day period were marked off by means of pure charcoal taken with the food at breakfast of the first day of each experiment and of the day following its completion. In order to minimize the danger of accidental contamination, the feces were usually received directly in platinum dishes and burned to ash without any previous manipulation. The nitrogen content of the feces was therefore not actually determined, but was estimated from the results of previous investigations.

PREPARATION AND SAMPLING OF FOOD MATERIALS.

The bread used in all these experiments was one of the common brands of biscuit or "soda crackers" sold in small sealed packages. The contents of several packages were mixed and sampled and portions weighed out for each day's dietary in advance.

In those experiments in which milk formed a part of the diet, it was obtained in sealed quart bottles from one of the large dealers in New York City and was doubtless from the mixed product of many

---

a U. S. Dept. Agr., Office Expt. Stas. Bul. 185.

cows. As a rule, a fresh bottle was opened at each meal, the contents thoroughly mixed, the specific gravity determined, and portions withdrawn at once for consumption and analysis. Since the specific gravity was found to be practically uniform, indicating that all the milk was of the same general quality, composite samples were prepared for analysis by mixing equal amounts from each bottle used.

Coagulated white of egg was used in the second experiment. This was obtained from eggs which had been kept in boiling water for about 30 minutes. The coagulated white of each egg was carefully removed and freed as thoroughly as possible from all traces of yolk or shell. Any dark specks noticed in the body of the white were also removed. The coagulated whites were then mixed in glass-stoppered bottles and portions were weighed for analysis and for each day's dietary.

METHODS OF ANALYSIS.

For the determination of moisture, fat, and ash the methods of the Association of Official Agricultural Chemists were used.[a] Nitrogen was determined by the Dyer modification of the Kjeldahl method, which has been found by repeated trials in this laboratory [b] to give slightly higher and more accurate results than those obtained by following exactly the directions of the official methods. Protein was estimated in all cases by multiplying the amounts or percentages of nitrogen by the factor 6.25. Phosphorus was determined by precipitating first as ammonium phosphomolybdate and finally as magnesium ammonium phosphate, organic matter having been destroyed before the first precipitation either by boiling with sulphuric and nitric acids, by burning with sodium carbonate (using nitrate if necessary to facilitate the oxidation), or in the case of feces, of which the ash was porous and alkaline, by simple ignition.

In the determination of calcium and magnesium in foods and feces the substances were burned in platinum and the ash dissolved in water and hydrochloric acid. To the solution ammonia was added until a permanent precipitate formed. Enough acetic acid was then added to just dissolve this precipitate, then also about 0.5 gram ammonium acetate; the solution was warmed and a saturated solution of ammonium oxalate added in slight excess, then allowed to stand 12 hours, filtered, and washed with water containing ammonium oxalate, ignited and weighed as CaO. The filtrate was then made slightly alkaline with ammonia, then hydrogen disodium phosphate added in slight excess, and allowed to stand in the cold for 1 hour. Then 10 cubic centimeters of 0.90 specific gravity ammonia were added for every 100 cubic centimeters of solution and

---

[a] U. S. Dept. Agr., Bur. Chem. Bul. 46, revised.
[b] Jour. Amer. Chem. Soc., 26 (1904), pp. 367, 1469.

allowed to stand overnight. The solution was filtered and the precipitate washed with 3 per cent ammonia solution, dried, separated from the paper, ignited, and weighed as $Mg_2P_2O_7$. In urine calcium and magnesium were determined by the usual gravimetric methods as given in Thierfelder's revision of Hoppe-Seyler's [a] volume on chemical analysis.

COMPOSITION OF FOOD MATERIALS.

The food materials used in the six metabolism experiments yielded, when analyzed by the methods above outlined, the following results:

Composition of food materials.

Laboratory No.	Food material.	Water.	Protein.	Fat.	Carbohydrates.	Calcium oxid.	Magnesium oxid.	Phosphorus.	Nitrogen.
		Per cent.	*P. ct.*	*P. ct.*	*Per cent.*	*Per cent.*	*P. ct.*	*P. ct.*	*P. ct.*
701	Crackers............	3. 55	9. 75	9. 95	75. 33	0. 0282	0. 0176	0. 0892	1. 56
702	Milk................	87. 04	3. 23	4. 11	4. 88	. 1739	. 0173	. 0941	. 517
703	Egg, white.........	86. 70	11. 13	. 27	....	. 0104	. 0170	. 0110	1. 78
831	Crackers............	5. 48	9. 70	9. 64	73. 80	. 0285	. 0173	. 0891	1. 552
832	Milk................	87. 14	3. 30	3. 89	4. 93	. 1729	. 0152	. 0944	. 528
833	Butter *a*...........	(*a*)	. 43	(*a*)	....	. 0216	. 0011	. 0136	. 069
834	Milk................	87. 40	3. 18	3. 91	4. 79	. 1635	. 0155	. 0944	. 508
835	.....do	87. 25	3. 23	3. 95	4. 86	. 1586	. 0156	. 0920	. 517

a The sample of butter was lost after determination of protein and mineral constituents, but before determinations of water and fat had been made. In calculating the fuel value of the diet in which butter was used it is assumed that the butter contained an average amount of fat and was of average fuel value.

DETAILS OF METABOLISM EXPERIMENT No. 1.

The experiment was begun at 7 a. m. December 30, 1905, and continued 3 days.

The weight of the subject (without clothing) was 65 kilograms (143 pounds) at the beginning and 62.5 kilograms (137.5 pounds) at the end of the experiment. It may be noted that the usual weight of this subject (without clothing) is 63 to 66 kilograms in winter and 60 to 63 kilograms in summer.

The daily food consisted of 150 grams of bread (crackers) and 1,500 grams of milk. The crackers furnished 14.6 grams protein, 14.9 grams fat, and 113 grams carbohydrates. The milk furnished 48.4 grams protein, 61.7 grams fat, and 73.2 grams carbohydrates. The total nutritive value of the diet was therefore 63 grams protein, 76.6 grams fat, and 186.2 grams carbohydrates, the fuel value being 1,690 calories.

---

[a] Hoppe-Seyler, Chemischen Analyse. Berlin, 1903, 7 ed., p. 346; 8 ed., 1909, p. 570.

227

The data regarding the income and outgo of mineral constituents and nitrogen are given in the following table:

Income and outgo of mineral constituents in metabolism experiment No. 1 (serial No. 11).

Kind of material.	Calcium oxid.	Magnesium oxid.	Phosphorus.	Nitrogen.
Food per day:	*Grams.*	*Gram.*	*Grams.*	*Grams.*
Bread (crackers)	0.042	0.026	0.134	2.34
Milk	2.609	.260	1.412	7.76
Total daily income	2.651	.286	1.546	10.10
Feces:				
Total, for 3 days	5.630	.510	1.710	(1.38)
Average per day	1.880	.170	.570	(.46)
Urine:				
First day (December 30 to January 1)			.850	12.52
Second day (January 1-2)			1.110	13.56
Third day (January 2-3)			1.140	13.19
Total, for 3 days	.630	.570	3.100	39.27
Average per day	.210	.190	1.030	13.09
Total outgo per day	2.090	.300	1.600	13.55
Gain (+) or loss (−) per day	+.561	−.074	−.054	−3.45

In this experiment, therefore, there was a considerable storage of calcium, slight losses of magnesium and phosphorus, and a considerable loss of nitrogen. The calcium, magnesium, and phosphorus balances will be discussed beyond in connection with those of the other experiments. The loss of nitrogen was due rather to the low fuel value than to the low protein of the diet, since experiment has shown that about 65 grams of protein suffice for the maintenance of nitrogen equilibrium in this subject when the food is of adequate fuel value.

DETAILS OF METABOLISM EXPERIMENT No. 2.

This experiment, which followed the preceding one without intermission, was begun at 7 a. m. January 3, 1906, and continued for 3 days.

The weight of the subject (without clothing) was approximately 62.5 kilograms (137.5 pounds) both at the beginning and at the end of the experiment.

The daily food consisted of 400 grams of bread (crackers) and 250 grams of coagulated white of egg. This food was taken with about 1,000 grams of distilled water. The crackers furnished 39 grams protein, 39.8 grams fat, and 301.3 grams carbohydrates. The egg white furnished 27.8 grams protein and 0.7 gram fat. The total nutritive value of the diet was therefore 66.8 grams protein, 40.5 grams fat, and 301.3 grams carbohydrates, the total fuel value being 1,833 calories.

227

The data recording the income and outgo of mineral constituents and nitrogen are given in the following table:

Income and outgo of mineral constituents in metabolism experiment No. 2 (serial No. 12).

Kind of material.	Calcium oxid.	Magnesium oxid.	Phosphorus.	Nitrogen.
Food per day:	*Grams.*	*Gram.*	*Grams.*	*Grams.*
Bread (crackers)	0.113	0.070	0.357	6.24
Egg white	.026	.043	.027	4.45
Total daily income [a]	.139	.113	.384	10.69
Feces:				
First day (January 3–4)	.480	.050	.170	....
Second day (January 4–5)	} .960	.190	.500	....
Third day (January 5–6)				
Total for 3 days	1.440	.240	.670	(2.25)
Average per day	.480	.080	.223	(.75)
Urine:				
First day (January 3–4)	....	....	.900	13.05
Second day (January 4–5)	....	....	.740	13.75
Third day (January 5–6)	....	....	.620	12.83
Total for 3 days	.290	.390	2.260	39.63
Average per day	.097	.130	.753	13.21
Total outgo per day	.577	.210	.976	13.96
Loss per day	.438	.097	.592	3.27

[a] About 1,000 grams of distilled water were taken daily with this diet.

The diet of the second experiment, while slightly higher in protein and fuel value than that of the first, contained only about one-twentieth as much lime, two-fifths as much magnesia, and one-fourth as much phosphorus. The diet (bread, egg white, and distilled water) was rather distasteful and appeared to be the cause of a slight looseness of the bowels, which appeared at the end of this period.

The balances show a moderate loss of magnesium and considerable losses of calcium, phosphorus, and nitrogen. At the close of this experiment the diet was increased to 2,560 calories with only a slight increase of protein, whereupon the loss of nitrogen fell at once to only 0.2 gram per day, showing that the negative nitrogen balance was attributable to insufficient fuel value.

DETAILS OF METABOLISM EXPERIMENT No. 3.

This experiment was begun at 7 a. m. June 3, 1906, and continued 3 days. In order that the bodily condition of the subject should be as nearly as possible the same as in the second experiment, the diet of the 3 days preceding the third experiment was the same as in the first experiment, viz, 150 grams of crackers and 1,500 grams of milk per day.

The weight of the subject (without clothing) was approximately 62.7 kilograms (138 pounds) at the beginning and 61.8 kilograms (136 pounds) at the end of the experiment. The initial weight was therefore practically the same in this as in the second experiment, and the loss of 0.9 kilogram during the 3 days was probably due as largely to the hot weather as to the deficient fuel value of the diet.

The daily diet consisted of 450 grams of the same lot of soda crackers as were used in the first and second experiments, with an average of 1,200 grams of distilled water per day. The crackers supplied 43.9 grams protein, 44.7 grams fat, and 339 grams carbohydrates, the total fuel value being 1,930 calories.

The average daily income and outgo of mineral constituents and nitrogen are shown in the following table:

Income and outgo of mineral constituents in metabolism experiment No. 3 (serial No. 13).

Kind of material.	Calcium oxid.	Magnesium oxid.	Phosphorus.	Nitrogen.
Food per day:	*Grams.*	*Gram.*	*Grams.*	*Grams.*
Bread (crackers)	0.126	0.079	0.401	7.02
Distilled water				
Total daily income	.126	.079	.401	7.02
Feces:				
Total for 3 days	3.690	.379	1.355	
Average per day	1.230	.126	.452	(.70)
Urine:				
First day (June 3–4)	.062	.086	.986	10.64
Second day (June 4–5)	.044	.095	.622	10.46
Third day (June 5–6)	.056	.098	.476	9.77
Total for 3 days	.162	.279	2.084	30.87
Average per day	.054	.093	.695	10.29
Total outgo per day	1.284	.219	1.147	10.99
Loss per day	1.158	.140	.746	3.97

Here, with the amounts of lime, magnesia, and phosphorus about the same as in the second experiment, the losses are in each case considerably greater and in the case of lime conspicuously so, the excretion of lime being more than twice as great as in the second experiment.

During this experiment the food did not become so distasteful as during the second, but there was some lack of appetite and at times a slight feeling of fullness and thirst after meals. There was also in this, as in the second experiment, a slight tendency toward looseness of the bowels.

DETAILS OF METABOLISM EXPERIMENT No. 4.

This experiment followed the preceding one without intermission and continued for 3 days, June 6–9, 1906.

The weight of the subject (without clothing) was approximately 61.8 kilograms (136 pounds) at the beginning and 63.2 kilograms (139 pounds) at the end of the experiment.

The diet consisted of 450 grams "soda crackers" (of the same kind as in the earlier experiments but from a different lot, No. 831), 450 grams milk (No. 832), 75 grams butter (No. 833), and 1,500 grams of hydrant water per day. The crackers furnished 43.7 grams of protein, 43.4 grams of fat, and 332 grams of carbohydrates. The milk furnished 14.9 grams of protein, 17.5 grams of fat, and 22 grams of carbohydrates. The butter furnished 0.3 gram protein and 63.8 grams of fat. The total food value was therefore 58.9 grams of protein, 124.7 grams of fat, and 354 grams of carbohydrates, yielding a total of 2,774 calories per day.

The data of income and outgo of calcium, magnesium, phosphorus, and nitrogen during this experiment are given in the following table:

Income and outgo of mineral constituents in metabolism experiment No. 4 (serial No. 14).

Kind of material.	Calcium oxid.	Magnesium oxid.	Phosphorus.	Nitrogen.
Food per day:	*Grams.*	*Gram.*	*Grams.*	*Grams.*
Bread (crackers)	0.128	0.078	0.401	6.98
Milk	.778	.068	.425	2.38
Butter	.017	.001	.010	.05
Water	.025	.013		
Total daily income	.948	.160	.836	9.41
Feces:				
Total for 3 days	2.147	.160	.678	
Average per day	.716	.053	.226	.77
Urine:				
First day (June 6–7)	.063	.102	.513	9.59
Second day (June 7–8)	.111	.139	.690	9.76
Third day (June 8–9)	.149	.155	.773	9.31
Total for 3 days	.323	.396	1.976	28.66
Average per day	.108	.132	.659	9.55
Total outgo per day	.824	.185	.885	10.32
Gain (+) or loss (—) per day	+.124	—.025	—.049	—.91

Here the fuel value of the diet was adequate and the subject was gaining in weight. The intake of 58.9 grams of protein, 0.836 gram of phosphorus (equivalent to 1.91 grams of P_2O_5), and 0.16 gram of magnesia was not quite sufficient for equilibrium, although in each case the body had received during the preceding period an even smaller allowance. A daily intake of 0.948 gram of lime resulted, however, in an average storage of 0.124 gram, or about one-eighth of the amount taken in the food.

DETAILS OF METABOLISM EXPERIMENT No. 5.

This experiment began on the morning of June 9, 1906, following experiment No. 4 without intermission, and continued for 3 days.

The weight of the subject (without clothing) was approximately 63.2 kilograms (139 pounds) at the beginning and 62.5 kilograms (137½ pounds) at the end of the experiment.

The diet consisted of 300 grams crackers (No. 831), 450 grams milk (No. 834), and 75 grams butter (No. 833) per day, with which was taken 1,000 cubic centimeters of hydrant water. The crackers furnished 29.1 grams protein, 28.9 grams fat, and 221 grams carbohydrates; the milk 14.3 grams protein, 17.6 grams fat, and 22 grams carbohydrates; the butter 0.3 gram protein and 63.8 grams fat. The total food was therefore 43.7 grams protein, 110.3 grams fat, and 243 grams carbohydrates, yielding in all 2,140 calories per day.

.The data of income and outgo of calcium, magnesium, phosphorus, and nitrogen are given for this period in the following table:

Income and outgo of mineral constituents in metabolism experiment No. 5 (serial No. 15).

Kind of material.	Calcium oxid.	Mag-nesium oxid.	Phos-phorus.	Nitrogen.
Food per day:	*Grams.*	*Gram.*	*Grams.*	*Grams.*
Bread (crackers)	0.096	0.052	0.267	4.66
Milk	.736	.070	.425	2.29
Butter	.017	.001	.010	.05
Water	.017	.009	....	....
Total daily income	.866	.132	.702	7.00
Feces:				
Total for 3 days	1.745	.138	.480	....
Average per day	.582	.046	.160	.54
Urine:				
First day (June 9–10)	.174	.116	.848	7.84
Second day (June 10–11)	.211	.155	.839	9.25
Third day (June 11–12)	.180	.144	.684	8.52
Total for 3 days	.565	.415	2.371	25.61
Average per day	.188	.138	.790	8.54
Total outgo per day	.770	.184	.950	9.08
Gain (+) or loss (−) per day	+.096	−.052	−.248	−2.08

Here, with a somewhat decreased intake of each of the elements studied as well as of the fuel value of the diet the storage of calcium continued at a somewhat decreased rate, and the losses of magnesium, phosphorus, and nitrogen continued at an increased rate as compared with the preceding experiment.

DETAILS OF METABOLISM EXPERIMENT No. 6.

This experiment followed that last described without intermission and continued for 3 days, June 12–15, 1906.

The weight of the subject was approximately 62.5 kilograms (137½ pounds) at the beginning and 62.3 kilograms (137 pounds) at the end of the experiment.

The diet consisted of 300 grams crackers (No. 831) and 1,350 grams milk (No. 835) per day. The crackers furnished 29.1 grams protein, 28.9 grams fat, and 221 grams carbohydrates; the milk, 43.6 grams protein, 53.3 grams fat, and 64 grams carbohydrates; the total food,

72.7 grams protein, 82.2 grams fat, and 285 grams carbohydrates; yielding in all 2,170 calories per day.

The data of income and outgo of calcium, magnesium, phosphorus, and nitrogen are given in the following table:

Income and outgo of mineral constituents in metabolism experiment No. 6 (serial No. 16).

Kind of material.	Calcium oxid.	Magnesi- um oxid.	Phos- phorus.	Nitrogen.
	Grams.	*Gram.*	*Grams.*	*Grams.*
Food per day:				
Bread (crackers)	0.096	0.052	0.267	4.66
Milk	2.141	.211	1.242	6.98
Total daily income	2.237	.263	1.509	11.64
Feces:				
Total for 3 days	5.420	.422	1.507	....
Average per day	1.807	.141	.502	(.68)
Urine:				
First day (June 12–13)	.301	.195	.988	10.70
Second day (June 13–14)	.322	.165	1.012	10.02
Third day (June 14–15)	.297	.177	.976	11.05
Total for 3 days	.920	.537	2.976	31.77
Average per day	.307	.179	.992	10.59
Total outgo per day	2.114	.320	1.494	11.27
Gain (+) or loss (−) per day	+.123	−.057	−.015	+.37

Here the fuel value was practically the same as in the preceding experiment, but the protein and ash constituents of the food were considerably increased. There was nearly constant body weight and approximate equilibrium of nitrogen and phosphorus and a small loss of magnesium. Although the calcium of the food was more than doubled, the amount stored in the body was but little increased, the output having risen with the intake, as might be expected, in view of the fact that the body was already sufficiently supplied, having received for six days previously somewhat more calcium than was actually required for the maintenance of equilibrium.

That the output of calcium can follow the intake so closely when more than the required amount is fed should tend to dispel any fear of an undue accumulation of lime in the body as the result of using food rich in calcium compounds.

COMPARISON OF BALANCES FOR LIME, MAGNESIA, AND PHOSPHORUS.

For convenience of comparison the lime, magnesia, and phosphorus balances for the 6 experiments are brought together in the table which follows.

227

Daily balances of income and outgo of lime, magnesia, and phosphorus.

Experiment No.	Calcium oxid.			Magnesium oxid.			Phosphorus.		
	Income.	Outgo.	Balance.	Income.	Outgo.	Balance.	Income.	Outgo.	Balance.
	Grams.	*Grams.*	*Grams.*	*Gram.*	*Gram.*	*Gram.*	*Grams.*	*Grams.*	*Gram.*
1.................	2.65	2.09	+0.56	0.29	0.36	−0.07	1.55	1.60	−0.05
2.................	.14	.58	− .44	.11	.21	− .10	.38	.97	− .59
3.................	.12	1.28	−1.16	.08	.22	− .14	.40	1.15	− .75
4.................	.94	.82	+ .12	.16	.19	− .03	.83	.88	− .05
5.................	.87	.77	+ .10	.13	.18	− .05	.70	.95	− .25
6.................	2.23	2.11	+ .12	.26	.32	− .06	1.51	1.49	+ .02

Assuming, as is customary in these investigations, that of any given element the "requirement" is the amount found by experiment to be sufficient for the maintenance of equilibrium under normal conditions, it is evident that since there was a loss of magnesium in each of the 6 experiments the magnesium requirement can not be deduced from them. It is also apparent that only those experiments in which there was a reasonably close approach to equilibrium of lime or of phosphorus can be taken as indicating the lime or phosphorus requirement.

Considering the great number of experiments which have been found necessary to establish the nitrogen requirement of man, it is evident that many more experiments should be made before attempting to draw conclusions regarding the requirements for calcium or for phosphorus. All that can be done at present is to point out the more obvious indications of the data now at hand.

CALCIUM REQUIREMENT.

In experiment No. 5 the body received 0.87 gram CaO and excreted only 0.77 gram, indicating that its requirement was not greater than the latter figure. On the other hand, in experiment No. 2, where the food furnished only 0.14 gram, the man nevertheless excreted 0.58 gram, indicating that at least the latter amount was required in his nutrition. These results therefore indicate that the lime requirement of this subject lay between 0.58 and 0.77 gram, though doubtless at other times and on other diets somewhat different figures might be obtained.

Among the earlier experiments reviewed above it is found that Bertram apparently required only 0.4 gram of CaO, and Gramatchikov also reports one case of equilibrium on 0.4 gram, while Renvall [a]

---

[a] From the data of one experimental day, which he believed to represent his requirement more accurately than the average, Renvall estimated his requirement at 0.95 gram CaO.

required 0.83 gram calcium equivalent to 1.16 grams CaO per day, and Von Wendt's requirement appeared to be somewhere between 0.4 and 0.85 gram CaO.

It appears, therefore, that a calcium requirement equivalent to about 0.7 gram CaO per day is indicated by the results of the present study and also approximates the average of earlier investigations, but further experiments are needed before any such estimate can be regarded as satisfactory. Experiments for this purpose must, of course, include a complete determination of the calcium balance, for while the amount of calcium found in the urine will usually be small it varies so greatly in absolute as well as in relative amount that no assumption regarding the distribution of calcium between feces and urine can be justified. In the experiments here reported from 3.9 to 23.7 per cent of the eliminated calcium appeared in the urine, but in one of Renvall's experiments the proportion was 64.3 per cent. In a large majority of the experiments by Renvall, Von Wendt, and the writers, the feces have contained between 60 and 90 per cent and the urine between 10 and 40 per cent of the eliminated calcium.

PHOSPHORUS REQUIREMENT.

In attempting to draw inferences in regard to the phosphorus requirement, greater difficulties are experienced than in the case of calcium. The closest agreement between income and outgo of phosphorus appears in the results for experiment No. 6, where there was equilibrium on 1.5 grams phosphorus per day. But in experiment No. 4 the same subject was very nearly in equilibrium when metabolizing only 0.88 gram per day. The requirement would therefore appear to lie anywhere between 0.9 and 1.5 grams. This wide variation is probably due in part at least to a difference in diet. In experiment No. 4 the phosphorus was obtained about equally from bread and from milk, while in experiment No. 6 more than four-fifths was derived from milk and less than one-fifth from bread. It is now believed that in bread nearly all of the phosphorus is in organic combination, while milk contains, in addition to its important organic compounds of phosphorus, a considerable proportion of simple phosphates. Since phosphorus appears to be of greater nutritive value in its organic than in its inorganic compounds, this is the probable explanation of the fact that much larger amounts of phosphorus were apparently required for approximate equilibrium in experiments Nos. 1 and 6 than in experiment No. 4.

. Doubtless, also, the previous habit of the subject plays a part in the metabolism of phosphorus, as it is well known to do in the metabolism of nitrogen. There might not have been such a close approach to equilibrium in experiment No. 4 if the subject had not been for some

227

days previously on food of low phosphorus content, and on the other hand the apparent phosphorus requirement of a man who had been living on a liberal mixed diet may be greater than the actual requirement as it would be found by gradually accustoming the subject to a diminished intake.

Hence an attempt to set a figure for the phosphorus requirement presents difficulties analogous to those surrounding the establishment of the protein requirement, and is rendered still more uncertain by the fact that much fewer experiments have been made upon the phosphorus metabolism than upon the metabolism of nitrogen. At present it can only be said that the data now available[a] indicate that a healthy man, by accustoming himself to a low phosphorus intake or by the selection of food containing phosphorus almost entirely in organic combination, may maintain equilibrium on a diet furnishing about 0.9 gram phosphorus, or about 2 grams P_2O_5, but that the maintenance of equilibrium at the normal level of a full diet, so as to insure the carrying of a full normal store of phosphorus compounds in the body, appears to call for the intake of about 1.5 grams of phosphorus, or about 3.5 grams of P_2O_5, per day.

Further experiments upon the phosphorus requirement are greatly needed, and these should be planned with due reference to the nature of the phosphorus compounds present in the different food materials. It need scarcely be added that these should be complete balance experiments, for in man the distribution of the eliminated phosphorus between urine and feces is so variable that no safe inferences regarding requirements can be drawn from any experiments except those in which the output by both feces and urine is accurately determined. Ehrström[b] has shown, by comparing the results of his own experiments upon phosphorus metabolism with those of Loewi[c] and Siven,[d] that in experiments with healthy men on normal diets the amount of phosphorus in the feces as compared with the amount in the food may vary at least from 12.2 to 71.8 per cent. In some of the experiments of Tigerstedt and Von Wendt, and in one of those here reported, the feces contained more phosphorus than the food. Of the total eliminated phosphorus in the six experiments here reported the feces contained 16.8 to 39.3 per cent and the urine 60.7 to 83.2 per cent.

---

[a] In addition to the experiments here reported the data of intake and output in about 75 earlier experiments have also been taken into account. Only a few of these, however, were arranged primarily with a view to the determination of the phosphorus requirement.

[b] Skand. Arch. Physiol., 14 (1903), p. 82.

[c] Arch. Expt. Path. u. Pharmakol., 45 (1900–1901), p. 157.

[d] Skand. Arch. Physiol., 11 (1901), p. 308.

CALCIUM, MAGNESIUM, AND PHOSPHORUS IN FOOD MATE-
RIALS AND IN TYPICAL AMERICAN DIETARIES.

In any general study of the food requirements of the human body it is important to supplement the results obtained from metabolism experiments by careful estimates of the actual amounts consumed by typical people living under normal conditions and with freely chosen food. In previous publications of this Office there have been given the detailed results of several hundreds of such dietary studies in which account was taken of the amounts of protein, fats, and carbohydrates consumed. In connection with a study of iron in food and its functions in nutrition, twenty of these dietaries were selected as typical, and the recorded data of food consumption were taken in connection with the recently determined percentages of iron in food materials as the basis of estimation of the actual amounts of food-iron in the ordinary diet of typical American families.

In a similar manner the calcium, magnesium, and phosphorus contents have now been estimated (1) of the same twenty typical family dietaries; (2) of 5 dietaries studied at the Maine State College in 1895[a] in cooperation with this Office, in which an attempt was made to control the sources of protein in the food consumed by a large college club; and (3) of an individual experimental dietary study made in New York City in 1906 in the course of the investigation upon iron in food and nutrition,[b] to which reference has already been made.

Comparatively few satisfactory data relating to the calcium, magnesium, and phosphorus contents of the edible portion of food material could be found, partly because the recorded analyses of food ash are sometimes of doubtful accuracy, but especially because ash analyses of food materials have most commonly been made by agricultural chemists, whose interest lay in determining the amounts of ash constituents removed from the soil by the crop, and who therefore analyzed the whole of the material removed from the soil or from the farm without always separating the edible from the inedible portion.

In order to guard against errors from such sources, ash analyses found in the literature have not been accepted in any important case without verification. One or more samples of each food material which furnishes an important proportion of the ash constituents of any given dietary has been analyzed in connection with this investigation, and the results thus obtained have been compared, and in most cases averaged, with any previously recorded results which appeared to be trustworthy. These results, which have been used in calculating the data of the dietary studies which are given in the table on page 41,

---

[a] U. S. Dept. Agr., Office Expt. Stas. Bul. 37.
[b] U. S. Dept. Agr., Office Expt. Stas. Bul. 185.

are therefore either the results of analyses made in connection with this study or are the average of data thus obtained and of such earlier data as appeared to be reasonably satisfactory.

In all cases in which it has been necessary to estimate the composition of dried or canned material from that of the corresponding fresh food, or vice versa, the computations have been based either upon moisture determinations made in the course of the analysis or upon the data contained in the standard compilation of analyses of American food materials.[a] In the case of jellies, jams, and other forms of fruits preserved with sugar, the ash contents have been assumed to average two-thirds as much as in the original fresh fruits.

The table which follows gives the data regarding the calcium, magnesium, and phosphorus content of food materials.

Ash constituents of food materials—Estimated average figures used in computing results of dietary studies.

Food materials.	Calcium oxid.	Magnesium oxid.	Phosphorus pentoxid.
ANIMAL FOODS, CEREALS, ETC.	*Per cent.*	*Per cent.*	*Per cent.*
Meats	(b)	(b)	(b)
Fish and shellfish	(c)	(c)	(c)
Eggs	0.100	0.015	0.367
Butter (and butterine)	.022	.001	.031
Buttermilk (estimated as milk)	.172	.018	.217
Cheese	1.240	.049	1.490
Cottage cheese	.100	.015	.455
Milk, condensed[d]	.430	.045	.542
Milk, whole	.172	.018	.217
Cream	.147	.015	.186
Barley, pearled	.025	.100	.460
Corn meal	.009	.132	.458
Hominy (as old process meal)	.014	.196	.708
Oatmeal (including rolled oats, etc.)	.078	.249	.974
Rice	.012	.060	.198
Wheat flour (crackers and macaroni)	.028	.026	.216
Ginger snaps (assumed)	.040	.030	.250
Graham flour and entire wheat flour (assumed)	.037	.150	.660
Flaked wheat breakfast food	.043	.239	.946
Bread used in dietary study No. 486	.082	.080	.279
Bread	.021	.019	.162
Chocolate	.141	.483	.897
Molasses	.355	.176	.132
Maple sirup	.123	.100	.100
Honey	.005	.030	.065
VEGETABLES.			
Asparagus	.038	.017	.094
Beans, pea, dried	.215	.252	1.098
Beans, kidney, dried	.226	.261	1.235
Beans, Lima, dried	.106	.311	.752
Beans, string, fresh	.073	.050	.091
Beets	.019	.029	.095
Cabbage	.058	.021	.081
Carrots	.077	.032	.094
Celery	.094	.027	.100
Corn, canned or green	.045	.070	.257
Cucumbers	.028	.018	.052
Eggplant	.017	.037	.079
Greens, turnip tops	.508	.036	.098

a U. S. Dept. Agr., Office Expt. Stas., Bul. 28, revised.

b Meats were estimated to contain per 100 grams protein, 0.076 gram CaO, 0.19 gram MgO, 2.3 grams P_2O_5.

c Fish and shellfish were estimated to contain per 100 grams protein, 0.18 gram CaO, 0.23 gram MgO, 2.8 grams P_2O_5.

d Estimated as equivalent to 2.5 times its weight of whole milk in ash constituents.

Ash constituents of food materials—Estimated average figures used in computing results of dietary studies—Continued.

Food materials.	Calcium oxid.	Magnesium oxid.	Phosphorus pentoxid.
VEGETABLES—continued.	*Per cent.*	*Per cent.*	*Per cent.*
Greens, soup greens (assumed)	0.080	0.030	0.085
Horseradish	.136	.038	.127
Lettuce	.045	.012	.073
Onions	.040	.015	.080
Parsnips	.076	.044	.183
Peas, dried	.137	.204	.855
Peas, canned	.023	.034	.142
Potatoes	.016	.040	.144
Potatoes, sweet	.025	.019	.080
Pumpkins	.032	.014	.135
Radishes	.025	.019	.070
Rhubarb	.060	.010	.103
Ruta-bagas	.103	.031	.129
Spinach	.064	.053	.103
Tomatoes	.019	.016	.045
Tomatoes, canned	.019	.016	.045
Turnips	.087	.029	.107
Vegetable soup (canned condensed)	.026	.021	.106
Water cress	.259	.046	.006
FRUITS.			
Apples	.011	.014	.026
Apples, evaporated	.037	.054	.121
Apricots	.021	.019	.058
Bananas	.009	.035	.061
Blackberries	.079	.037	.083
Blueberries	.045	.015	.046
Cherries	.026	.027	.075
Cranberries	.021	.012	.034
Currants	.016	.026	.070
Currants, dried	.169	.076	.178
Dates	.104	....	.122
Figs, dried	.280	.144	.332
Grapes	.014	.019	.065
Grape jelly	.009	.015	.043
Grape fruit	.029	.015	.043
Huckleberries	.037	.027	.070
Oranges	.043	.016	.048
Peaches, dried	.048	.093	.334
Peaches	.015	.015	.049
Pears	.018	.014	.041
Pears, canned	.008	.007	.020
Pineapples	.038	.027	.022
Plums	.022	.019	.038
Plums, jam, canned	.014	.012	.025
Prunes	.063	.084	.204
Raisins	.042	.070	.240
Raspberries	.072	.037	.093
Strawberries	.057	.036	.068
Watermelons	.018	.022	.034
MISCELLANEOUS.			
Pie, apple (assumed)	.030	.030	.100
Pie, cream (assumed)	.040	.030	.150
Pie, custard (assumed)	.060	.030	.200
Pie, mince	.044	.037	.191
Pie, squash	.030	.015	.150

DIETARY STUDIES IN PROFESSIONAL MEN'S FAMILIES.

DIETARY STUDY OF A LAWYER'S FAMILY IN PITTSBURG (NO. 43).[a]

This study was made in the winter of 1895 in the family of a lawyer in comfortable circumstances, and continued 30 days. The family consisted of 2 men, 6 women, a girl 12 years old, and frequent visitors.

---

[a] For full data regarding the amount and composition of the food eaten, see U. S. Dept. Agr., Office Expt. Stas. Bul. 52, p. 12.

The total number of meals taken was estimated as equivalent to those of one man for 227 days, and the total food eaten, calculated per man per day, furnished 91 grams of protein and 3,280 calories at a cost of 22.3 cents.

In calculating the amounts consumed per man per day in the different dietaries, use has been made in all cases of the conventional assumption as to the relative amounts of food eaten by women and children as compared with men. These have been summarized in an earlier publication.[a]

The table below shows the kinds and amounts of foods used, together with the estimated amounts of lime, magnesia, and phosphoric anhydrid furnished by each and by the diet as a whole.

Estimated ash constituents in dietary study No. 43.

Food materials and weight of edible portion.	Calcium oxid.	Magnesium oxid.	Phosphorus pentoxid.
	Grams.	*Grams.*	*Grams.*
Meats: Beef, veal, lamb, and pork (total meat protein, 7,900 grams)..	6.004	15.010	181.700
Salmon, 1,215 grams (164 grams protein)	.295	.377	4.590
Eggs, 10,775 grams	10.775	1.616	39.544
Butter, 13,510 grams	2.972	.135	4.188
Cheese, 625 grams	7.750	.306	9.312
Milk, 55,725 grams	95.847	10.030	120.923
Cream, 18,305 grams	26.908	2.745	34.047
Barley, 365 grams	.091	.365	1.679
Flour and macaroni, 52,500 grams	14.700	13.650	113.400
Corn meal, 3,940 grams (new process)	.354	5.200	18.045
Oatmeal, 3,090 grams	2.410	7.694	30.096
Rice, 1,520 grams	.182	.912	.300
Bread, 5,105 grams	1.072	.909	8.270
Sugar, 23,250 grams			
Molasses, 3,175 grams	11.271	5.588	4.191
Beans, Lima, dried, 1,275 grams	1.351	3.965	9.588
Beans, pea, dried, 3,035 grams	6.525	7.648	33.324
Cabbage, 1,930 grams	1.119	.405	1.563
Corn, canned, 1,825 grams	.821	1.277	4.690
Lettuce, 285 grams	.128	.034	.208
Onions, 535 grams	.214	.080	.428
Peas, canned, 5,175 grams	1.190	2.759	7.348
Potatoes, 35,855 grams	5.736	14.342	51.631
Potatoes, sweet, 3,795 grams	.948	.721	3.036
Tomatoes, canned, 6,045 grams	1.148	.967	2.720
Oranges, 2,440 grams	1.049	.390	1.171
Cranberries, 1,475 grams	.309	.177	.501
Prunellas (as prunes), 905 grams	.570	.760	1.846
In total food	201.739	98.122	688.339
In waste (7 per cent)	14.119	6.869	48.183
In total food eaten	187.620	91.253	640.156
Per man per day	.83	.40	2.82

DIETARY STUDY OF A TEACHER'S FAMILY IN INDIANA (NO. 44).[b]

This study was made in March, 1895, and continued 14 days. The family consisted of 4 men and 2 women. One of the men was a professor of mathematics, 1 an instructor in chemistry, the other 2 were college students. The younger woman was also a teacher. The total food consumed was equivalent to that of 1 man for 78 days. The

---

[a] U. S. Dept. Agr., Farmers' Bul. 142, p. 33.

[b] U. S. Dept. Agr., Office Expt. Stas. Bul. 32, p. 12.

food eaten furnished 106 grams of protein and 2,780 calories, at a cost of 18 cents per man per day.

The table below shows the kinds and amounts of foods used, together with the estimated amounts of lime, magnesia, and phosphoric anhydrid furnished by each and by the diet as a whole.

Estimated ash constituents in dietary study No. 44.

Food materials and weight of edible portion.	Calcium oxid.	Magnesium oxid.	Phosphorus pentoxid.
	Grams.	*Grams.*	*Grams.*
Meats: Beef, veal, pork, and lamb (total meat protein, 3,413 grams)	2.593	6.484	78.499
Eggs, 4,705 grams	4.705	.705	17.267
Butter, 1,785 grams	.392	.017	.543
Milk, 55,055 grams	94.694	9.909	119.469
Mince-meat, 370 grams	.162	.136	....
Corn meal, 2,395 grams	.215	3.161	10.969
Hominy, 255 grams (as old-process corn meal)	.033	.499	1.805
Flour and crackers, 14,625 grams	4.095	3.802	31.590
Oatmeal, 240 grams	.187	.597	2.337
Sugar, 6,605 grams	....	....	....
Maple sirup, 895 grams	1.100	.895	.895
Honey, 425 grams	.021	.127	.276
Beans, dried, 835 grams	1.795	2.104	9.168
Cabbage, 2,890 grams	1.676	.606	2.340
Corn, canned, 1,210 grams	.544	.847	3.109
Lettuce, 905 grams	.407	.108	.660
Parsnips, 795 grams	.604	.349	1.454
Potatoes, 6,750 grams	1.080	2.700	9.720
Radishes, 310 grams	.077	.058	.217
Apples, 5,470 grams	.601	.765	1.422
Bananas, 1,420 grams	.127	.497	.866
Cranberries, 355 grams	.074	.042	.120
Oranges, 540 grams	.232	.086	.259
Peaches, dried, 865 grams	.415	.804	2.889
Prunes, dried, 865 grams	277	.369	.897
Raisins, 45 grams	.018	.031	.108
In total food	116.124	35.698	296.879
In waste (4.3 per cent)	4.902	1.535	12.767
In food eaten	111.132	34.163	284.112
Per man per day	1.42	.44	3.64

DIETARY STUDY OF A SCHOOL SUPERINTENDENT'S FAMILY IN CHICAGO (NO. 91).[a]

This study was made in April and May, 1895, and covered 14 days. The family consisted of 1 man, 4 women (3 of whom were teachers), 2 children 8 and 2 years old, and occasional visitors. The total food consumed was equivalent to that of 1 man for 75 days. The food eaten per man per day furnished 123 grams protein and 3,260 calories, at a cost of 33.6 cents.

The table following shows the kinds and amounts of foods used, together with the estimated amounts of lime, magnesia, and phosphoric anhydrid furnished by each and by the diet as a whole.

[a] U. S. Dept. Agr., Office Expt. Stas. Bul. 55, pp. 66, 67.

Estimated ash constituents in dietary study No. 91.

Food materials and weight of edible portion.	Calcium oxid.	Magnesium oxid.	Phosphorus pentoxid.
	Grams.	*Grams.*	*Grams.*
Meats: Beef, veal, lamb, and chicken (total meat protein, 4,275 grams)	3.249	8.122	98.325
Fish, 2,040 grams (225 grams protein)	.405	.517	6.300
Eggs, 5,555 grams	5.555	.833	20.386
Butter, 4,320 grams	.950	.043	1.339
Cheese, 455 grams	5.642	.222	6.779
Milk, 25,400 grams	43.688	4.572	55.118
Cream, 3,175 grams	4.667	.476	5.905
Corn meal, 2,710 grams (new process)	.243	3.577	12.331
Flour, crackers, and macaroni, 16,785 grams	4.700	4.364	36.255
Sugar, 4,535 grams			
Molasses, 225 grams	.798	.396	.297
Asparagus, 340 grams	.129	.057	.319
Beans, string, 1,130 grams	.824	.565	.102
Cucumbers, as purchased, 4,990 grams	1.397	.898	2.594
Lettuce, 455 grams	.204	.054	.332
Onions, 455 grams	.182	.068	.364
Peas, fresh, 1,475 grams	.516	.752	3.200
Potatoes, as purchased, 27,215 grams	4.354	10.886	39.189
Radishes, 455 grams	.113	.086	.318
Tomatoes, 1,820 grams	.345	.291	.419
Bananas, as purchased, 6,125 grams	.551	2.143	3.736
Lemons, as purchased, 2,040 grams	.877	.326	.979
Prunes, dried, 455 grams	.286	.382	.928
Strawberries, 4,080 grams	2.325	1.468	2.770
In total food	82.000	41.098	298.289
Per man per day (making no allowance for waste)	1.09	.55	3.97
Per man per day (allowing 10 per cent for waste)	.98	.50	3.58
Per man per day (allowing 5 per cent for waste)	1.04	.52	3.78

DIETARY STUDY OF A TEACHER'S FAMILY IN NEW YORK (NO. 485).[a]

This study began with breakfast December 8, 1905, and covered 10 days. The family consisted of 1 man, 3 women (1 of whom was a colored servant at active muscular work), and a child 16 months old. The total number of meals taken was estimated as equivalent to the food consumption of 1 man at teacher's occupation for 39 days. The food eaten furnished 102 grams of protein and 3,184 calories, at a cost of 29.4 cents per man per day.

The table following shows the kinds and amounts of foods used, together with the estimated amounts of lime, magnesia, and phosphoric anhydrid furnished by each and by the diet as a whole.

[a] U. S. Dept. Agr., Office Expt. Stas. Bul. 185, p. 60.

Estimated ash constituents in dietary study No. 485.

Food materials and weight of edible portion.	Calcium oxid.	Magnesium oxid.	Phosphorus pentoxid.
	Grams.	*Grams.*	*Grams.*
Meats: Beef, 4,550 grams, pork and lard, 1,020 grams (total meat protein, 860 grams)	0.653	1.634	19.780
Codfish, 567 grams (protein, 95 grams)	.171	.213	2.660
Eggs, 2,920 grams	2.920	.438	10.716
Milk, 26,310 grams	45.253	4.738	57.092
Butter, 2,040 grams	.448	.020	.632
Cheese, 455 grams	5.642	.222	6.779
Bread, 7,120 grams, buns, 200 grams	1.537	1.390	11.858
Flour, 1,905 grams, crackers, 365 grams, macaroni, 135 grams	.673	.625	5.194
Ginger snaps, 270 grams, cookies, 90 grams	.144	.108	.900
Corn meal, 225 grams	.020	.297	1.030
Hominy, 113 grams	.015	.221	.800
Oatmeal, 905 grams	.705	2.253	8.814
Rice, 55 grams	.006	.033	.108
Sugar, 2,595 grams			
Molasses, 410 grams	1.455	.721	.541
Beans, Lima, dried, 200 grams	.212	.622	1.504
Beans, pea, dried, 425 grams	.913	1.071	4.666
Beans, string, 965 grams	.704	.482	.878
Corn, sweet, dried, 115 grams	.182	.280	1.069
Lettuce, 255 grams	.114	.030	.186
Peas, dried, 90 grams	.123	.183	.769
Potatoes, 6,395 grams	1.023	2.558	9.208
Potatoes, sweet, 1,360 grams	.340	.258	1.088
Turnips, 1,725 grams	1.500	.500	1.845
Apples, fresh, 1,645 grams	.180	.230	.427
Apples, evaporated, 225 grams	.083	.121	.272
Bananas, 1,065 grams	.095	.372	.649
Grape jelly, 400 grams	.036	.060	.172
Orange, 75 grams	.032	.012	.136
Prunes, 565 grams	.355	.474	1.152
Raisins, 600 grams	.252	.420	1.440
Chocolate, 65 grams	.091	.313	.583
Olive oil, 70 grams			
In total food eaten	65.878	20.918	152.848
Per man per day	1.69	.54	3.92

DIETARY STUDIES OF COLLEGE STUDENTS' CLUBS.

DIETARY STUDY OF A STUDENTS' CLUB, UNIVERSITY OF TENNESSEE (NO. 207).[a]

This study was made during 14 days in November, 1896, in a university boarding club. The group consisted of 90 men (2 professors, 87 students, and a servant), 9 women, of whom 5 were servants, and 1 child 10 years of age. The total food consumption was equivalent to that of 1 man for 1,278 days. The food eaten per man per day furnished 123 grams protein and 3,595 calories, at a cost of 18 cents.

The table following shows the kinds and amounts of foods used, together with the estimated amounts of lime, magnesia, and phosphoric anhydrid furnished by each and by the diet as a whole.

---

[a] U. S. Dept. Agr., Office Expt. Stas. Bul. 53, p. 19.

Estimated ash constituents in dietary study No. 207.

Food materials used.	Calcium oxid.	Magnesium oxid.	Phosphorus pentoxid.
	Grams.	*Grams.*	*Grams.*
Meat: Beef, veal, pork, fowl (total meat protein, 81 kilograms)	61.5	153.9	1,863.0
Fish: Catfish, salmon (total fish protein, 6.6 kilograms)	11.8	15.1	184.8
Eggs, 56.05 kilograms	56.0	8.4	
Butter, 75.64 kilograms	16.6	.7	23.4
Milk, 636 kilograms	1,094.1	114.4	1,380.1
Corn meal, 42.4 kilograms	3.8	55.9	194.6
Corn meal, grits and hominy (as old-process meal), 10.9 kilograms	1.5	21.3	77.1
Oatmeal, 42.9 kilograms	33.4	106.8	417.8
Graham flour, 6.9 kilograms	2.5	10.3	45.5
Flour and crackers, 189.3 kilograms	53.0	49.2	408.8
Rice, 10.7 kilograms	1.2	6.4	21.1
Bread, 50.2 kilograms	10.5	9.5	81.3
Chocolate, 1.47 kilograms	2.0	7.1	13.1
Sugar, 164.4 kilograms			
Molasses, 36.3 kilograms	128.8	63.8	47.9
Cornstarch and tapioca, 4.8 kilograms			
Beans, dried, 6.35 kilograms	13.6	16.0	69.7
Cabbage, 25.3 kilograms	14.6	5.3	20.4
Celery, 0.905 kilogram	.8	.2	.9
Lettuce, 11.7 kilograms	5.2	1.4	8.5
Potatoes, 134.3 kilograms	21.4	53.7	193.3
Sweet potatoes, 87.2 kilograms	21.8	16.5	69.7
Turnips, 24.5 kilograms	21.3	7.1	26.2
Tomatoes, canned, 36.9 kilograms	7.0	5.9	16.6
Corn, canned, 8.6 kilograms	3.8	6.0	22.1
Pickles and chowder, 29 kilograms	8.1	5.2	15.0
Apples, 98.5 kilograms	10.8	13.7	25.6
Cranberries, 4.8 kilograms	1.0	.5	1.6
Bananas, 5.1 kilograms	.4	1.7	3.1
Currants, dried, 0.68 kilogram	1.1	.5	1.2
Figs, 5.5 kilograms	15.4	7.9	18.2
Grapes, 18.4 kilograms	2.5	3.4	11.9
Peaches and pears, canned, 24.8 kilograms	2.2	2.3	6.4
Apricots, peaches, and pears, evaporated, 10.03 kilograms	80.8	85.5	275.5
Oranges, 1.02 kilograms	.4	.1	.4
Prunes, dried, 7.37 kilograms	4.6	6.2	15.0
In total food purchased	1,713.5	861.9	5,559.8
In waste (7 per cent)	119.9	60.3	389.1
In total food eaten	1,593.6	801.6	5,170.7
Per man per day	1.25	.63	4.05

DIETARY STUDY OF WOMEN STUDENTS, PAINESVILLE, OHIO (NO. 323).[a]

This study covered 10 days of January, 1900. The group studied consisted of 115 women, of whom 20 were instructors, 91 students, and 4 servants. The total meals taken were equivalent to the food of 1 woman for 1,049 days. "The attempt was made to regulate the diet in such a way that it should not exceed a definite cost and at the same time please the students." The food eaten per woman per day furnished on an average 68 grams protein and 2,665 calories, at a cost of 18.3 cents.

The table following shows the kinds and amounts of foods used, together with the estimated amounts of lime, magnesia, and phosphoric anhydrid furnished by each and by the diet as a whole.

---

[a] For full data regarding the amount and composition of the food eaten, see U. S. Dept. Agr., Office Expt. Stas. Bul. 91, p. 30.

Estimated ash constituents in dietary study No. 323.

Food materials used.	Calcium oxid.	Magnesium oxid.	Phosphorus pentoxid.
	Grams.	*Grams.*	*`- Grams.*
Meat: Beef, mutton, pork, chicken (total meat protein, 33.6 kilograms)	25.5	63.8	772.8
Fish and oysters (protein 1.06 kilograms)	1.9	2.4	29.6
Eggs, 13 kilograms	13.0	1.9	47.7
Butter, 60.5 kilograms	13.3	.6	18.7
Cheese, 5.78 kilograms	71.6	2.8	8.6
Milk, 322.7 kilograms	554.0	58.0	700.2
Cream, 5.45 kilograms	8.0	.8	10.1
Corn meal, 11.8 kilograms	1.0	15.5	54.0
Hominy, 2.7 kilograms	.3	5.2	19.1
Wheat breakfast food (as Graham flour) 15.1 kilograms	5.5	22.6	99.6
Graham flour, 33.7 kilograms	12.4	50.5	222.2
Rice, 7 kilograms	.8	4.2	13.8
Whole wheat flour, 3.27 kilograms	1.2	4.9	21.5
Flour and crackers, 142 kilograms	39.7	36.9	306.7
Sugar, 74.9 kilograms			
Cornstarch, 0.8 kilogram			
Tapioca, 1.8 kilograms			
Molasses, 6.6 kilograms	23.4	11.6	8.7
Maple sirup, 7.9 kilograms	9.7	7.9	7.9
Chocolate, 1.1 kilograms	1.5	5.3	9.8
Beans, Lima, dried, 4.9 kilograms	5.1	15.2	36.8
Beans, pea, dried, 6.7 kilograms	14.4	16.8	73.5
Beets, 14.1 kilograms	2.6	4.0	13.3
Cabbage, 4.5 kilograms	2.6	.9	3.6
Parsnips, 15.9 kilograms	12.0	6.9	29.0
Peas, canned, 10.3 kilograms	2.3	3.5	15.6
Peas, dried, 2 kilograms	2.7	4.0	17.1
Potatoes, 139 kilograms	22.2	55.6	61.1
Sweet potatoes, 16.6 kilograms	4.1	3.1	13.2
Spinach, 5.14 kilograms	3.2	2.7	5.2
Squash, 5.14 kilograms	5.3	2.3	22.6
Tomatoes, 11.1 kilograms	2.1	1.7	4.9
Turnips, 14.5 kilograms	13.6	4.2	15.5
Cucumbers, pickles, 4.3 kilograms	1.2	.7	2.2
Apples, 44.3 kilograms	4.8	6.2	11.5
Apricots, 5.2 kilograms	1.0	.9	3.0
Apple butter, 13.8 kilograms	1.5	1.9	3.5
Bananas, 30 kilograms	2.7	10.5	18.3
Cherries, canned 4.5 kilograms	.7	.8	2.2
Cranberry sauce, 11.8 kilograms	1.6	.9	2.7
Dates, 8.8 kilograms	9.1	193.1	10.7
Figs, 1.4 kilograms	3.9	2.0	4.6
Lemons, 2.7 kilograms	1.1	.4	1.2
Oranges, 68.2 kilograms	29.3	10.9	32.7
Prunes, 4.9 kilograms	3.0	4.1	9.9
Raisins, 0.7 kilogram	.2	.4	1.6
Raspberry jam, 6.4 kilograms	3.0	1.6	3.9
In total food	938.1	650.2	2,780.4
In waste (13 per cent)	121.9	84.5	361.4
In total food eaten	816.2	565.7	2,419.0
Per woman per day	.78	.54	2.30
Estimated per man per day	.97	.67	2.88

DIETARY STUDIES OF MECHANICS' AND INDOOR LABORERS' FAMILIES.

DIETARY STUDY OF A CARPET DYER'S FAMILY IN NEW YORK (NO. 35).[a]

This study was made in April and May, 1895, and covered 10 days. The group consisted of the family and 3 boarders, and included 4 men, 1 woman, 3 boys (aged 12, 7, and 3 years), and 6 girls (aged 14, 11, 6, 4, and 2 years, and 8 months). The woman did sewing, and the 14-year-old girl did the marketing and housekeeping. The total meals taken were equivalent to the meals of 1 man for 92 days. The food eaten

[a] U. S. Dept. Agr., Office Expt. Stas. Bul. 46, pp. 23, 78.

cost 16 cents and furnished 71 grams of protein and 2,430 calories per man per day.

The table below shows the kinds and amounts of foods used, together with the estimated amounts of lime, magnesia, and phosphoric anbydrid furnished by each and by the diet as a whole.

Estimated ash constituents in dietary study No. 35.

Food materials used.	Calcium oxid.	Magnesium oxid.	Phosphorus pentoxid.
	Grams.	*Grams.*	*Grams.*
Meat: Beef, pork, and chicken (total meat protein, 2,685 grams)....	2.040	5.101	61.755
Fish: Cod, salmon, and sardines (total fish protein, 400 grams)......	.720	.920	11.200
Eggs, 3,445 grams..	3.445	.516	12.643
Butter, 3,530 grams...	.798	.036	1.125
Cheese, 410 grams...	5.084	.200	6.109
Milk, 11,725 grams	20.167	2.110	25.443
Condensed milk, 455 grams...	1.956	.204	2.466
Barley (pearled), 680 grams..	.170	.680	3.128
Flour, crackers, and macaroni, 2,635 grams.........................	.737	.685	5.691
Oatmeal, 1,360 grams..	1.060	3.386	13.264
Bread, 23,845 grams	5.007	4.530	38.628
Rice, 410 grams...	.049	.246	.811
Sugar, 6,850 grams, tap'oca, 455 grams.............................	....	....	....
Cabbage sprouts, 1,770 grams......................................	1.416	.531	1.504
Onions, 2,765 grams...	1.106	.414	2.212
Potatoes, 15,865 grams..	2.538	6.346	22.845
Soup greens, 170 grams..	.136	.051	.144
Jam, 575 grams...	.080	.069	.143
Plums, canned, 225 grams..	.031	.027	.056
Prunes, dried, 680 grams...	.428	.571	1.387
Raisins, 455 grams..	.191	.318	1.092
In total food...	47.160	26.941	211.626
In waste (1.2 per cent)..	.565	.323	2.539
In total food eaten..	46.595	26.618	209.087
Per man per day..	.501	.289	2.273

DIETARY STUDY OF A TIN ROOFER'S FAMILY IN NEW YORK CITY (NO. 112).[a]

This study was made during 11 days in November, 1895. The group comprised the family proper and 3 boarders. It was considered a typical Irish-American family. Five men and 4 women were included in the study, the son and daughters being grown. The total meals taken were equivalent to the meals of 1 man for 93 days. The food purchased, which was all eaten, furnished per man per day 84 grams of protein and 2,335 calories, at a cost of 16 cents.

The table following shows the kinds and amounts of foods used, together with the estimated amounts of lime, magnesia, and phosphoric anhydrid furnished by each and by the diet as a whole.

---

[a] U. S. Dept. Agr., Office Expt. Stas. Bul. 46, pp. 59, 109.

Estimated ash constituents in dietary study No. 112.

Food materials used.	Calcium oxid.	Magnesium oxid.	Phosphorus pentoxid.
	Grams.	*Grams.*	*Grams.*
Meat: Beef and pork (total meat protein, 4,170 grams)	3.169	7.923	95.910
Fish: Fresh and salt cod (total fish protein, 205 grams)	.369	.471	5.740
Eggs, 3,285 grams	3.285	.492	12.055
Butter, 3,200 grams	.704	.032	.992
Milk, 14,235 grams	24.484	2.562	30.880
Oatmeal, 905 grams	.705	2.253	8.814
Rice, 230 grams	.027	.138	.455
Bread, 17,500 grams	3.675	3.325	28.350
Sugar, 5,615 grams			
Cabbage, 7,175 grams	3.161	1.506	5.811
Corn, canned, 910 grams	.409	.637	2.338
Onions, 905 grams	.362	.135	.724
Peas, canned, 905 grams	.208	.307	1.285
Potatoes, 21,800 grams	3.488	8.720	31.802
In total food eaten	44.046	28.501	224.755
Per man per day	.47	.30	2.41

DIETARY STUDY OF A SEWING WOMAN'S FAMILY IN NEW YORK CITY (NO. 48).[a]

This study was made during 7 days of June, 1895. The family consisted of the mother, 5 sons aged 14, 11, 8, 4, and 3 years, and 1 daughter, 6 years old. The total food consumption was equivalent to that of 1 man for 28 days. The income of the family was only $30 to $40 a month, of which $10 was paid for rent. As the mother was the principal wage-earner, it was impossible to give much time to the purchasing and preparation of the food. The cost per person per day was less than 6 cents, calculated per man per day, 9 cents. The food eaten furnished per man per day 54 grams of protein and 1,500 calories.

The table below shows the kinds and amounts of foods used, together with the estimated amounts of lime, magnesia, and phosphoric anhydrid furnished by each and by the diet as a whole.

Estimated ash constituents in dietary study No. 48.

Food materials used.	Calcium oxid.	Magnesium oxid.	Phosphorus pentoxid.
	Grams.	*Grams.*	*Grams.*
Meat: Beef and pork (total meat protein, 170 grams)	0.129	0.323	3.910
Fish: Sardines (protein, 58 grams)	.104	.133	1.624
Eggs, 1,625 grams	1.625	.243	5.963
Butter, 225 grams	.049	.002	.080
Milk, 8,390 grams	14.430	1.510	18.206
Barley (pearled), 340 grams	.085	.340	1.564
Bread, rolls, and cake, 3,685 grams	.773	.700	5.969
Flour and crackers, 1,815 grams	.508	.471	3.920
Sugar, 1,735 grams			
Beans, dried, 905 grams	1.945	2.280	9.936
Potatoes, 1,815 grams	.290	.726	2.613
Radishes, 285 grams	.071	.054	.199
Rhubarb, 180 grams	.108	.018	.185
Tomatoes, canned, 1,135 grams	.215	.181	.510
In total food purchased	20.336	6.981	54.668
In waste (6 per cent)	1.220	.418	3.280
In total food eaten	19.116	6.563	51.388
Per man per day	.682	.234	1.835

a U. S. Dept. Agr., Office Expt. Stas. Bul. 46, pp. 33, 86.

DIETARY STUDY OF A HOUSE DECORATOR'S FAMILY IN PITTSBURG (NO. 190).[a]

This study was made during 30 days in January and February, 1897, in a family consisting of 1 man, 1 woman, a girl of 15, and 2 boys, 12 and 2 years old. The meals taken were estimated as equivalent to those of 1 man for 96 days. The income was estimated as $84 per month, and as the result of good management in the marketing a considerable variety of both animal and vegetable foods was obtained. The food eaten furnished per man per day 112 grams of protein and 3,305 calories, at a cost of 19.6 cents.

The table below shows the kinds and amounts of foods used, together with the estimated amounts of lime, magnesia, and phosphoric anhydrid furnished by each and by the diet as a whole.

Estimated ash constituents in dietary study No. 190.

Food materials used.	Calcium oxid.	Magnesium oxid.	Phosphorus pentoxid.
	Grams.	*Grams.*	*Grams.*
Meat: Beef, veal, lamb, pork (total meat protein, 5,495 grams)	4.176	10.440	126.385
Oysters (protein, 36 grams)	.064	.082	1.008
Eggs, 1,875 grams	1.875	.281	6.881
Butter, 2,995 grams	.638	.029	.928
Milk, 32,590 grams	56.054	5.866	70.720
Barley (pearled), 285 grams	.071	.285	1.311
Corn meal, 940 grams	.084	1.240	4.305
Flour and crackers, 19,680 grams	5.510	5.116	42.508
Rice, 255 grams	.030	.153	.504
Bread and cake, 5,345 grams	1.101	.996	8.496
Beans, dried, 1,375 grams	2.956	3.455	15.097
Beets, 3,090 grams	.587	.896	2.935
Cabbage, 5,895 grams	3.419	1.237	4.774
Corn, canned, 1,770 grams	.079	1.239	4.548
Onions, 200 grams	.080	.030	.160
Peas, canned, 595 grams	.136	.202	.844
Pickles, 765 grams (as cucumbers)	.214	.137	.397
Potatoes, sweet, 4,155 grams	1.038	.789	3.324
Potatoes, 21,625 grams	3,460	8.650	31.140
Soup greens, 15 grams	.012	.004	.012
Turnips, 2,905 grams	2.527	.842	3.108
Catsup, 300 grams (as tomato)	.057	.048	.135
Chili sauce, 965 grams (as tomato)	.183	.154	.484
Sauerkraut, 1,335 grams (as cabbage)	.774	.280	1.081
Apples, 22,985 grams	2.528	3.217	5.976
Bananas, 2,730 grams	.245	.955	1.655
Oranges, 1,010 grams	.434	.161	.484
Lemons, 260 grams	.111	.041	.124
Peaches, canned, 1,940 grams	.194	.232	.620
Plum butter, 3,315 grams (as plums)	.729	.629	1.259
In total food	89.386	47.696	341.153
In waste (3.2 per cent)	2.860	1.526	10.916
In food eaten	86.526	46.170	330.237
Per man per day	.901	.480	3.439

[a] U. S. Dept. Agr., Office Expt. Stas. Bul. 52, p. 31.

227

DIETARY STUDY OF A GLASS BLOWER'S FAMILY IN PITTSBURG (NO. 191).[a]

This study was made in a family of adults, 4 men and 3 women, in January and February, 1897, and covered 31 days, during which the total number of meals taken was equivalent to the meals of 1 man for 186 days. Two of the men were idle at the time of the study. The food eaten furnished per man per day 94 grams of protein and 3,085 calories, at a cost of 16 cents.

The table below shows the kinds and amounts of foods used, together with the estimated amounts of lime, magnesia, and phosphoric anhydrid furnished by each and by the diet as a whole.

Estimated ash constituents in dietary study No. 191.

Food materials used.	Calcium oxid.	Magnesium oxid.	Phosphorus pentoxid.
	Grams.	*Grams.*	*Grams.*
Meat: Beef, veal, lamb, pork, chicken (total meat protein, 8,537 grams)	6.488	16.220	196.351
Fish (protein, 287 grams)	.516	.660	8.036
Eggs, 3,995 grams	3.995	.599	14.661
Butter, 6,675 grams	41.047	4.295	51.787
Cottage cheese, 2,520 grams	2.520	.378	11.466
Corn meal, 1,375 grams	.123	1.815	6.297
Flour and crackers, 40,960 grams	11.468	10.649	88.473
Oatmeal, 880 grams	.686	2.191	8.571
Rice, 555 grams	.066	.333	1.098
Bread and cake, 9,765 grams	2.050	1.855	15.819
Sugar, 18,345 grams, cornstarch, 40 grams			
Beans, dried, Lima, 1,300 grams	1.378	4.043	9.776
Corn, canned, 625 grams	.281	.437	1.606
Celery, 325 grams	.305	.087	.325
Onions, 2,255 grams	.902	.338	1.804
Potatoes, 34,350 grams	5.496	13.740	49.464
Potatoes, sweet, 2,995 grams	.748	.569	2.396
Tomatoes, canned, 3,835 grams	.728	.613	1.725
Turnips, 4,335 grams	3.771	1.257	4.638
Catsup, 2,710 grams (as tomatoes)	.514	.433	1.219
Pickles, 425 grams (as cucumbers)	.119	.076	.221
Sauerkraut, 2,780 grams (as cabbage)	1.612	.583	' 2.251
Vegetable soup, 3,855 grams	1.002	.809	21.281
Apples, 18,780 grams	2.065	2.629	4.882
Bananas, 780 grams	.070	.273	.475
Figs, dried, 610 grams	1.708	.878	2.025
Lemons, 60 grams	.025	.009	.028
Peaches, dried, 225 grams	.108	.209	.751
Jelly and jam, 1,785 grams	.249	.214	.446
Apples, fresh, and tomato butter, 2,355 grams	.259	.329	.672
In total food	91.767	66.587	510.613
In waste (0.7 per cent)	.642	.466	3.574
In food eaten	91.125	66.121	507.039
Per man per day	.489	.355	2.726

DIETARY STUDY OF A MILL WORKMAN'S FAMILY IN PITTSBURG (NO.128).[b]

This study was made during 29 days of January and February, 1896, in a family consisting of 2 men, 1 woman, 2 girls aged 16 and 6, and 3 boys aged 13, 10, and 8 years, respectively, the total food eaten being equivalent to the meals of 1 man for 167 days. This

---

[a] U. S. Dept. Agr., Office Expt. Stas. Bul. 52, p. 35.
[b] U. S. Dept. Agr., Office Expt. Stas. Bul. 52, p. 18.

family was taken as representative of a large class of poor foreign laborers in Pittsburg. The food eaten, calculated per man per day, cost 13 cents, and furnished 83 grams of protein and 2,525 calories.

The table below shows the kinds and amounts of foods used, together with the estimated amounts of lime, magnesia, and phosphoric anhydrid furnished by each and by the diet as a whole.

Estimated ash constituents in dietary study No. 128.

Food materials used.	Calcium oxid.	Magnesium oxid.	Phosphorus pentoxid.
	Grams.	*Grams.*	*Grams.*
Meat: Beef and pork (total meat p tein, 5,685 grams)	4.320	10.821	130.755
Fish: Herring and salmon (total fish protein, 708 grams)	1.274	1.628	19.824
Eggs, 2,735 grams	2.735	.410	10.037
Butter, 5,480 grams	1.205	.054	1.698
Cheese, 740 grams	9.176	.362	11.026
Milk, 19,305 grams	33.204	3.474	41.891
Barley, 255 grams	.063	.255	1.173
Flour, 21,555 grams	.715	.664	5.518
Oatmeal, 455 grams	.354	1.132	4.431
Rice, 455 grams	.054	.273	.900
Bread and cake, 46,960 grams	9.861	8.942	76.075
Pie, mince, 2,585 grams	1.137	.956	4.937
Sugar, 8,210 grams			
Molasses, 1,755 grams	6.230	3.088	2.316
Beans, dried, 2,350 grams	5.052	5.922	25.803
Peas, dried, 115 grams	.157	.234	.983
Onions, 1,205 grams	.482	.180	.964
Potatoes, 48,335 grams	7.733	19.334	69.602
Tomatoes, canned and catsup, 1,835 grams	.348	.293	.825
Apples, 1,020 grams	.112	.142	.265
Jam, 570 grams	.079	.068	.142
Prunes, 400 grams	.252	.336	.816
In total food	84.543	58.568	409.981
In waste (1.8 per cent)	1.522	1.054	8.380
In food eaten	83.021	57.514	401.601
Per man per day	.50	.34	2.40

DIETARY STUDY OF A MILL WORKMAN'S FAMILY IN PITTSBURG (NO. 129).[a]

This study was begun in January, 1896, and continued 29 days. The family consisted of 2 men, 2 women, and 5 children, aged, respectively, 13, 10, 7, and 4 years, and 7 months. The family was in very poor circumstances. The total number of meals taken was calculated by the usual factors as equivalent to the meals of 1 man for 174 days. The food furnished per man per day 77 grams protein and 2,440 calories, at a cost of 8.7 cents.

The table following shows the kinds and amounts of foods used, together with the estimated amounts of lime, magnesia, and phosphoric anhydrid furnished by each and by the diet as a whole.

---

[a] U. S. Dept. Agr., **Office Expt. Stas. Bul. 52, p. 22.**

Estimated ash constituents in dietary study No. 129.

Food materials used.	Calcium oxid.	Magnesium oxid.	Phosphorus pentoxid.
	Grams.	*Grams.*	*Grams.*
Meat: Beef and pork (total meat protein, 5,350 grams).............	4.066	10.165	123.050
Oysters (protein, 32 grams)...........................	.057	.073	.896
Butterine, 3,910 grams (as butter).......................	.860	.039	1.212
Cheese, 1,860 grams................................	23.064	.911	27.714
Milk, 14,745 grams.................................	25.361	2.654	31.996
Flour, 9,810 grams.................................	2.746	2.550	20.189
Oatmeal, 285 grams................................	.222	.709	2.775
Bread, cake, and rolls, 52,075 grams....................	....	....	....
Pie, 3,720 grams...................................	....	....	....
Sugar, 10,455 grams................................	....	....	....
Beans, dried, 580 grams.............................	1.247	1.461	6.368
Beans, dried, Lima, 1,330 grams......................	1.409	4.136	10.001
Cabbage, 4,590 grams..............................	2,662	.963	3.717
Carrots, 670 grams................................	.515	.214	.629
Celery, 200 grams.................................	.188	.054	.200
Onions, 3,445 grams...............................	1.378	.516	2.756
Parsnips, 655 grams...............................	.497	.288	1.198
Potatoes, 21,215 grams.............................	3.394	8.086	30.549
Watercress, 115 grams.............................	.297	.052	.075
Ruta-bagas, 2.180 grams............................	1.264	.457	1.765
Apples, 1,715 grams...............................	.188	.240	.445
Apple jelly, 365 grams.............................	.025	.032	.062
In total food...................................	69.440	33.600	265.597
In waste (0.6 per cent)..........................	.416	.201	1.593
In food eaten..................................	69.024	33.399	264.004
Per man per day...............................	.396	.192	1.517

DIETARY STUDY OF A MECHANIC'S FAMILY IN KNOXVILLE, TENN. (NO. 181).[a]

The family here studied consisted of 1 man, 2 women, and a boy 11 years old. The man was an engineer at hard work. The study covered 14 days in February, 1896. The total number of meals taken was equivalent to the food of 1 man for 48 days. The food eaten furnished per man per day 97 grams of protein and 4,060 calories, at a cost of 12 cents.

The table below shows the kinds and amounts of foods used, together with the estimated amounts of lime, magnesia, and phosphoric anhydrid furnished by each and by the diet as a whole.

Estimated ash constituents in dietary study No. 181.

Food materials used.	Calcium oxid.	Magnesium oxid.	Phosphorus pentoxid.
	Grams.	*Grams.*	*Grams.*
Meats: Pork and chicken (total meat protein, 1,380 grams).........	1.048	2.622	31.740
Butter, 1,590 grams................................	.349	.015	.492
Buttermilk (as milk), 9,070 grams......................	15.600	1.632	19.681
Eggs, 1,135 grams.................................	1.135	.170	4.165
Corn meal, 14,720 grams............................	1.324	19.430	67.417
Flour, 9,410 grams................................	2.634	2.446	20.325
Sugar, 455 grams..................................	....	....	....
Beans, dried, 1,815 grams...........................	3.902	4.673	19.928
Peas, dried, 905 grams.............................	1.239	1.846	7.737
Onions, 680 grams................................	.272	.102	.544
Turnip greens, 3,630 grams.........................	18.440	1.306	3.557
Potatoes, 8,255 grams.............................	1.320	3.302	11.887
Fruit jelly, 1,700 grams............................	.153	.255	.731
In total food...................................	47.416	37.799	188.204
In waste (8.6 per cent)..........................	4.077	3.250	16.185
In food eaten..................................	43.339	34.549	172.019
Per man per day...............................	.902	.719	3.581

a U. S. Dept. Agr., Office Expt. Stas. Bul. 53, p. 15.

DIETARY STUDIES OF FARMERS' FAMILIES AND OUTDOOR LABORERS.

DIETARY STUDY OF MAINE LUMBERMEN (NO. 391).[a]

This study was begun in January, 1902, and continued 16 days. The group included 30 men, most of whom were engaged in severe outdoor labor. The total number of meals taken was equivalent to the meals of 1 man for 492 days. The food eaten furnished per man per day 179 grams of protein and 6,780 calories, at a cost of 23.6 cents.

The table below shows the kinds and amounts of foods used, together with the estimated amounts of lime, magnesia, and phosphoric anhydrid furnished by each and by the diet as a whole.

Estimated ash constituents in dietary study No. 391.

Food materials used.	Calcium oxid.	Magnesium oxid.	Phosphorus pentoxid.
	Grams.	*Grams.*	*Grams.*
Meat: Beef, pork, and sausage (total meat protein, 35.2 kilograms)...	26.752	66.880	809.610
Fish: Cod, mackerel, and salmon (total fish protein, 9 kilograms)...	16.200	20.700	252.000
Butter, 20.9 kilograms	4.598	.209	6.479
Condensed milk, 1.4 kilograms	6.020	.630	7.588
Lard compound, 64.8 kilograms			
Corn meal, 5.7 kilograms	.513	7.524	26.106
Oatmeal, 0.9 kilogram	.702	2.241	8.766
Rice, 3.6 kilograms	.432	2.160	7.128
Flour, 173.6 kilograms	48.608	45.136	374.976
Sugar, 63 kilograms			
Molasses, 68.2 kilograms	242.110	120.032	90.024
Beans, dried, 101.6 kilograms	218.440	256.032	1,115.568
Carrots, 5.5 kilograms	4.235	1.760	5.170
Peas, dried, 4.5 kilograms	6.165	9.180	38.475
Potatoes, 78 kilograms	12.480	31.200	112.320
Onions, 0.2 kilogram	.080	.030	.160
Turnips, 28.6 kilograms	24.882	8.294	30.602
Apples, dried, 18.4 kilograms	6.808	9.936	22.264
Prunes, 28 kilograms	17.640	23.520	57.120
Raisins, 4.5 kilograms	1.890	3.150	10.800
Currant jelly, 7.5 kilograms	2.400	1.275	3.525
Strawberry jelly, 8.4 kilograms	3.192	2.016	3.780
In total food	644.147	611.905	2,982.461
In waste (3 per cent)	19.324	18.357	89.473
In food eaten	624.823	593.548	2,892.988
Per man per day	1.269	1.206	5.880

DIETARY STUDY OF A FARMER'S FAMILY IN CONNECTICUT (NO. 45).[b]

This study was made in December, 1894, and continued 7 days. The family consisted of 2 men, 1 woman, a boy 7 years old, a girl 4 years old, and a child under 2 years. The total number of meals taken was equivalent to the meals of 1 man for 27 days. The food furnished 108 grams protein and 3,548 calories per man per day.

The table following shows the kinds and amounts of food used, together with the estimated amounts of lime, magnesia, and phosphoric anhydrid furnished by each and by the diet as a whole.

---

[a] U. S. Dept. Agr., Office Expt. Stas. Bul. 149, p. 17.
[b] Connecticut Storrs Sta. Rpt. 1895, p. 148.

Estimated ash constituents in dietary study No. 45.

Food materials used.	Calcium oxid.	Magnesium oxid.	Phosphorus pentoxid.
	Grams.	*Grams.*	*Grams.*
Meat: Beef, lard, and chicken (protein, 671 grams)	0.509	1.274	15.433
Milk, 9,000 grams	15.480	1.620	19.530
Butter, 455 grams	.100	.004	.141
Flour, 12,700 grams	3.556	3.302	27.432
Sugar, 2,040 grams			
Cabbage, 3,630 grams	2.105	.762	2.940
Potatoes, 8,095 grams	1.295	3.238	11.656
Pumpkins, 4,535 grams	1.451	.634	6.122
Squash, 680 grams	.217	.095	.918
Sweet potatoes, 3,175 grams	.793	.603	2.540
Turnips, 4,765 grams	4.145	1.381	5.098
Apples, 13,260 grams	1.458	1.856	3.447
In total food eaten	31.109	14.769	95.257
Per man per day	1.152	.547	3.528

DIETARY STUDY OF A FARMER AND MECHANIC'S FAMILY IN TENNESSEE (NO. 182).[a]

This study was made during 14 days in March, 1896, in a family consisting of 3 men and 3 women, the total meals taken being equivalent to the meals of 1 man for 66 days. The food eaten furnished 95 grams of protein and 2,820 calories at a cost of 19 cents per man per day.

The table below shows the kinds and amounts of foods used, together with the estimated amounts of lime, magnesia, and phosphoric anhydrid furnished by each and by the diet as a whole.

Estimated ash constituents in dietary study No. 182.

Food materials used.	Calcium oxid.	Magnesium oxid.	Phosphorus pentoxid.
	Grams.	*Grams.*	*Grams*
Meat: Beef and pork (total meat protein, 2,250 grams)	1.710	4.275	51.750
Fish (protein, 279 grams)	.502	.641	7.812
Eggs, 5,605 grams	5.605	.840	20.600
Butter, 1,980 grams	.435	.019	.613
Milk and buttermilk, 16,950 grams	29.154	3.051	36.781
Flour and crackers, 10,525 grams	2.947	2.736	22.734
Oatmeal, 2,435 grams	1.899	6.063	23.716
Rice, 565 grams	.067	.339	1.118
Sugar, 1,130 grams			
Maple sirup, 680 grams	.836	.680	.680
Tapioca, 115 grams			
Beans, dried, 3,705 grams	7.965	9.336	40.680
Cabbage, 1,300 grams	.788	.285	1.101
Corn, canned, 7,470 grams	3.361	5.229	19.197
Parsnips, 1,020 grams	.775	.448	1.866
Potatoes, 20,035 grams	3.205	8.014	28.850
Tomatoes, canned, 765 grams	.145	.122	.344
Raisins, 285 grams	.119	.199	.684
Canned huckleberries, 6,705 grams	1.609	1.206	3.084
In total food	61.122	43.483	261.610
In waste (10 per cent)	6.112	4.348	26.161
In food eaten	55.010	39.135	235.449
Per man per day	.83	.59	3.56

a U. S. Dept. Agr., Office Expt. Stas. Bul. 53, p. 16.

DIETARY STUDY OF FARM STUDENTS AT KNOXVILLE, TENN. (NO. 208).[a]

The group included in this study consisted of 13 men whose ages averaged 25.4 years, 5 women whose average age was 32 years, and 1 child 7 years old. The study covered 14 days in December, 1896, the total meals taken being equivalent to the meals of 1 man for 155 days. The rate of board was $2 per week. The food actually eaten per man per day furnished 66 grams of protein and 3,560 calories at a cost of 15 cents.

The table below shows the kinds and amounts of foods used, together with the estimated amounts of lime, magnesia, and phosphoric anhydrid furnished by each and by the diet as a whole.

Estimated ash constituents in dietary study No. 208.

Food materials used.	Calcium oxid.	Magnesium oxid.	Phosphorus pentoxid.
	Grams.	*Grams.*	*Grams.*
Meats: Beef, pork, lard, fowl (total meat protein, 2,470 grams)	1.877	4.693	56.810
Eggs, 1,995 grams	1.995	.299	7.321
Butter, 7,005 grams	1.541	.070	2.171
Milk and buttermilk, 26,820 grams	46.130	4.827	58.199
Corn meal, 2,720 grams	.244	3.590	12.457
Corn meal grits, 3,430 grams	.480	6.722	24.284
Flour and crackers, 46,490 grams	3.719	12.087	100.418
Oatmeal, 3,005 grams	2.343	7.482	29.268
Rice, 3,400 grams	.408	2.040	6.732
Bread and cake, 5,390 grams	1.131	1.024	8.731
Sugar, 12,930 grams			
Molasses, 1,390 grams	4.934	2.446	1.834
Cabbage, 4,650 grams	2.697	.976	3.766
Celery, 1,135 grams	1.066	.306	1.135
Onions, 595 grams	.238	.089	.476
Sweet potatoes, 1,885 grams	.471	.358	1.508
Potatoes, 19,730 grams	3.156	7.892	28.411
Radishes, 340 grams	.085	.064	.238
Turnips, 3,175 grams	2.762	.920	3.397
Apples, 6,720 grams	.739	.940	1.747
Cranberries, 1,505 grams	.316	.180	.511
Canned grapes and blackberries, 4,085 grams	1.245	.775	2.001
Preserved plums, 5,870 grams	.821	.704	1.467
In total food	78.398	58.484	352.882
In waste (8.6 per cent)	6.742	5.029	30.348
In food eaten	71.656	53.455	322.534
Per man per day	.46	.34	2.08

DIETARY STUDY OF A NEGRO FARMER'S FAMILY IN ALABAMA (NO. 139).[b]

This family consisted of 1 man and 1 woman. The study was begun in January, 1896, and continued 16 days. The food taken was estimated to be equivalent to the meals of 1 man 29 days. The man and wife lived in a one-room cabin and worked a 25-acre farm, which was part of a large plantation about 7 miles from Tuskegee. They were in more comfortable circumstances than most negro farmers of the region. They expended for food about 10 cents per day

---

[a] U. S. Dept. Agr., Office Expt. Stas. Bul. 53, p. 21.
[b] U. S. Dept. Agr., Office Expt. Stas. Bul. 38, p. 56.

and obtained (on the same basis) 80 grams of protein and 4,955 calories.

The table below shows the kinds and amounts of foods used, together with the estimated amounts of lime, magnesia, and phosphoric anhydrid furnished by each and by the diet as a whole:

Estimated ash constituents in dietary study No. 139.

Food materials used.	Calcium oxid.	Magnesium oxid.	Phosphorus pentoxid.
	Grams.	*Grams.*	*Grams.*
Meat: Pork, bacon, and lard (total meat protein, 683 grams)	0.519	1.297	15.709
Milk, 1,020 grams	1.754	.183	2.213
Corn meal, 13,610 grams	1.224	17.905	62.333
Flour, 5,245 grams	1.468	1.363	11.329
Rice, 595 grams	.714	.357	1.178
Sugar, 1,030 grams			
Sweet potatoes, 1,985 grams	.496	.377	1.588
In total food	6.175	21.542	94.350
Per man per day	.213	.742	3.253

DIETARY STUDY OF A NEGRO FARMER'S FAMILY IN ALABAMA (NO. 100).[a]

This study was made at the same time and in the same region as the one preceding. The family consisted of a man and wife and 5 children, the eldest of whom was 11 years old; total consumption of food being equivalent to the meals of 1 man 59 days. The food furnished 44 grams of protein and 2,240 calories at a cost of 3 cents per man per day.

The table below shows the kinds and amounts of foods used, together with the estimated amounts of lime, magnesia, and phosphoric anhydrid furnished by each and by the diet as a whole:

Estimated ash constituents in dietary study No. 100.

Food materials used.	Calcium oxid.	Magnesium oxid.	Phosphorus pentoxid.
	Grams.	*Grams.*	*Grams.*
Meat: Bacon and lard (meat protein, 131 grams)	0.099	0.248	3.013
Flour, 9,470 grams	2.651	2.462	20.455
Corn meal, 20,920 grams	1.882	27.614	95.813
Rice, 710 grams	.085	.426	1.405
Collards, 255 grams (as cabbage)	.147	.053	.206
In total food eaten	4.864	30.803	120.892
Per man per day	.082	.522	2.049

If it be assumed that old-process corn meal was used, the estimated ash constituents would in this case be considerably higher.

---

[a] U. S. Dept. Agr., Office Expt. Stas. Bul. 38, p. 28.

DIETARIES IN WHICH THE SOURCE OF PROTEIN WAS CONTROLLED.[a]

Dietaries No. 148 to 152 differ from the other 20 included in this study in that they were not simply observations upon freely chosen food. In 4 of these 5 dietaries attempts were made to influence the food supply, especially the foods which furnish the greater part of the protein. The following extract from the original description of these studies shows the questions which they were designed to solve and the general conditions under which observations were made:

It has been repeatedly demonstrated on the basis of chemical analyses and market prices that the edible dry matter of oysters, clams, poultry, and the choice cuts of beef has a market cost much greater than that of the edible dry matter from a forequarter of beef or from pork, milk, and cheese. Consequently the housewife and boarding-house steward are assured that there is opportunity of keeping down the cost of supplying the table by purchasing those materials which furnish a unit of nutrition for the least money, provided they can be prepared for the table in such palatable forms that they are relished, and eaten without excessive waste.

It is quite evident, however, that these conditions are more difficult in the concrete than in the abstract. The lack of culinary skill, the necessity for a desirable variety of foods, and the marked differences of individual tastes are all obstacles to the easy application of laboratory demonstrations to the management of a dietary.

It was felt that if these views of food economics could be made useful in practice it would be well worth while to show this by accurate experimental data. It was decided, therefore, that nothing could be undertaken more desirable from a practical standpoint than to attempt an application of the considerations above mentioned. * * *

The college boarding house [in which these studies were made] is connected with the dormitory and is patronized chiefly by the students living in the dormitory and the neighboring fraternity clubhouses. Certain members of the college faculty and a few outside students take their dinners at the boarding house regularly and others occasionally, thus making a larger number of dinners than of other meals. The regular student boarders were, with a single exception, all young men whose ages ranged from 17 to 23 years, and who weighed on an average about 150 pounds. They were all compelled to take a fair amount of physical exercise, due to enforced military drill and to afternoon practice work in the laboratories, and with engineering instruments in the field. It may be reasonably claimed that these young men performed a considerable amount of work. There were also several women boarders and employees who had meals regularly at the commons. * * * The general plan of the studies may be briefly outlined as follows: At the beginning of each dietary study a careful inventory by weight was taken of all the food and food materials in the house. During the experimental period all food purchased was weighed and recorded in the same way, and all table and kitchen waste carefully collected, weighed, and dried for subsequent analysis. * * *

In these dietary studies, as already stated, the attempt was made to deliberately control to some extent the source and supply of animal foods. The object of this control was to bring into comparison high-cost and low-cost foods as a source of protein, with especial attention to the influence of the free use of milk as a low-cost animal food upon the character and cost of the dietary.

Milk was selected for special consideration for the following reasons: (1) Milk has a widespread use as an article of diet, and in all civilized countries is an important item of food supply. (2) Milk is a very valuable food.' It contains a mixture of the three classes of nutrients in forms that are readily digested and assimilated. (3) Milk is a low-cost animal food in proportion to its value, as based upon chemical analysis. It is shown * * * that when milk is purchased at $2 per 100 pounds the cost of a pound of edible solids is 15.7 cents, while the cost of a pound of edible solids in beef at $10.50 per 100 pounds is 34.3 cents. This is a comparison of the retail cost of milk with the cost of hind-quarter beef when purchased by the carcass. Beef bought as steak at retail prices would have a much higher comparative cost. (4) Notwithstanding the high quality and very general distribution of milk as a food, it seems by many to be regarded as a luxury, in the purchase of which economy must be exercised. This attitude toward this particular food may in part be explained by the somewhat prevalent notion that a free supply of milk in the dietary is not economical, because it is supposed that as much of other foods is eaten as would be the case if milk were not taken. This belief runs contrary to certain generally accepted facts which relate to the physiological use of foods and it only remains for experimental data to prove or disprove its correctness. Again, milk is not given full credit by people at large for its true nutritive value. Surprise is generally occasioned by the statement that a quart of milk has approximately the food value of a pound of steak. It is important to demonstrate, for reasons of economy, whether, as is the custom with many, it is wise to purchase the least possible quantity of milk and exercise little care in buying meats.

To investigate these questions, five dietary studies were made. In the first no change was made from the ordinary condition of living; in the second the protein was derived chiefly from high-priced animal foods, and the supply of milk was limited; in the third protein was derived from cheaper sources and milk was very abundantly supplied; in the fourth and fifth no departure was made from the ordinary conditions except in the amount of milk supplied—in the fourth the milk supply being limited and in the fifth very abundant.

DIETARY UNDER ORDINARY CONDITIONS (NO. 148).[a]

The study began February 24, 1895, and continued 58 days. The total number of meals taken by men was 12,238 and by women 793. Total equivalent to 1 man for 4,344 days. The food eaten furnished per man per day 132 grams of protein and 4,990 calories at a cost of 26 cents

The table following shows the kinds and amounts of foods used, together with the estimated amounts of lime, magnesia, and phosphoric anhydrid furnished by each and by the diet as a whole.

---

[a] U. S. Dept. Agr., Office Expt. Stas. Bul. 37, p. 26.

Estimated ash constituents in dietary study No. 148.

Food materials used.	Calcium oxid.	Magnesium oxid.	Phosphorus pentoxid.
	Grams.	Grams.	Grams.
Meat: Beef, veal, mutton, pork, poultry (total meat protein, 237.2 kilograms)	180.272	450.680	5,455.600
Fish: Cod, haddock, halibut, shad, clams, oysters (total fish protein, 43 kilograms)	77.400	98.900	1,204.000
Eggs, 229.5 kilograms	229.500	34.425	842.265
Butter, 225.8 kilograms	49.676	2.258	69.998
Milk, 3,953.1 kilograms	6,799.332	711.558	8,578.227
Gelatine, 1 kilogram			
Corn meal, 65.5 kilograms	5.895	86.460	299.990
Hominy, 27.7 kilograms	3.878	46.813	196.116
Flour, crackers, macaroni, 1,802.8 kilograms	504.784	468.728	3,894.048
Graham flour, 30.8 kilograms	11.396	46.200	203.280
Oatmeal, 49.2 kilograms	38.376	122.508	479.208
Rice, 2.3 kilograms	.276	1.380	4.554
Brown bread, 407 kilograms	9.768	40.700	179.000
Cake, frosted, 2.3 kilograms	.483	.437	3.726
Cookies, 1.6 kilograms	.336	.304	2.692
Pie, cream, 1 kilogram	.300	.300	1.000
Pie, mince, 5 kilograms	2.200	1.850	9.550
Pie, squash, 22.2 kilograms	6.660	3.330	33.300
Cornstarch, 3.2 kilograms			
Tapioca, 3.6 kilograms			
Chocolate, 2.3 kilograms	3.243	11.109	20.631
Sugar, 1,093.6 kilograms			
Molasses, 202.1 kilograms	717.455	355.696	266.772
Maple sirup, 321.4 kilograms	395.322	321.400	321.400
Beans, 104.8 kilograms	225.320	264.096	1,150.704
Beans, cooked, 9.5 kilograms	9.690	11.400	49.780
Beets, 11.6 kilograms	21.204	32.364	106.025
Cabbage, 112.5 kilograms	65.250	23.625	91.125
Carrots, 2.3 kilograms	1.771	.736	2.162
Onions, 37.2 kilograms	14.880	5.580	29.760
Parsnips, 22.1 kilograms	16.796	9.724	40.443
Peas, 4.5 kilograms	6.165	9.180	38.475
Peas, canned, 56 kilograms	12.880	19.040	79.520
Potatoes, 1,425.7 kilograms	228.112	570.280	2,053.008
Potatoes, cooked, 11.1 kilograms	2.131	5.328	19.179
Pumpkins, canned, 20.65 kilograms	6.416	2.807	27.067
Salad, 1.36 kilograms (as lettuce)	.612	.163	.992
Squash, 123.4 kilograms	39.488	27.276	166.690
Squash, canned, 23.7 kilograms	7.584	3.318	31.995
Tomatoes, canned, 24.5 kilograms	4.655	3.920	11.025
Turnips, 226.3 kilograms	196.881	65.627	242.141
Horse-radish, 10.7 kilograms	14.552	4.066	2.889
Catsup, 6 kilograms (as tomatoes)	1.140	.960	2.700
Cucumber pickles, 22.7 kilograms	6.356	4.106	11.804
Apples, evaporated, 10.4 kilograms	3.848	5.616	12.584
Apricots, dried, 6.8 kilograms	6.664	6.052	18.496
Crab apples, canned, 32.2 kilograms	.225	.289	.547
Blackberries, canned, 10.4 kilograms	5.408	2.392	5.720
Blueberries, canned, 26.2 kilograms	7.860	2.620	8.122
Currants, dried, 6.4 kilograms	10.816	4.864	11.392
Lemons, whole, 26 kilograms	11.180	4.160	12.480
Oranges, whole 45.4 kilograms	19.522	7.264	21.692
Pineapples, canned, 10 kilograms	2.500	1.800	1.400
Prunes, 11.3 kilograms	7.119	9.492	23.052
Prunes, cooked, 1.4 kilograms	.252	.336	.854
Raisins, 20.8 kilograms	8.736	14.560	49.920
In total food	10,002.565	3,928.077	26,289.100
In cooked food not eaten and in waste (23 per cent)	2,300.589	903.457	6,046.493
In food eaten	7,701.976	3,024.620	20,242.607
Per man per day	1.773	.696	4.659

DIETARY CONTAINING EXPENSIVE PROTEIN (NO. 149).[a]

In the second dietary study changes were made in the ordinary diet. Protein was supplied from expensive sources with a view to determining the effect on the amount and cost of the nutrients actually consumed. The matron was given the following instructions: Select animal food as far as possible from the following sources:

---

[a] U. S. Dept. Agr., Office Expt. Stas. Bul. 37, p. 30.

Hindquarter of beef, lamb, veal, chicken, eggs, halibut, salmon, shad, and lobster. During this period it is desirable that milk shall be served but once a day and that meat shall be used as freely as practicable, not only for dinner, but also for breakfast and supper. It is desired that meat shall be consumed in this period as freely as is consistent with health with a consequent diminishing of cereals and vegetable foods. Beans need not be served in this period unless in order to satisfy the boarders.

The study began April 24, 1895, and continued 26 days. Total meals taken by men, 4,011; by women, 310. Total equivalent to 1 man for 1,440 days.

The food eaten during this period furnished 112 grams of protein and 4,105 calories at a cost of 34 cents per man per day.

The table below shows the kinds and amounts of foods used, together with the estimated amounts of lime, magnesia, and phosphoric anhydrid furnished by each and by the diet as a whole.

Estimated ash constituents in dietary study No. 149.

Food materials used.	Calcium oxid.	Magnesium oxid.	Phosphorus pentoxid.
	Grams.	*Grams.*	*Grams.*
Meat: Beef, veal, mutton, pork, poultry (total meat protein, 95.1 kilograms)	72.276	180.690	2,187.300
Fish: Bluefish, cod, halibut, shad, lobster (total fish protein, 22.5 kilograms)	40.500	51.750	630.000
Eggs, 160.3 kilograms	160.300	24.045	588.301
Butter, 118.4 kilograms	26.049	1.184	36.704
Milk, 1,165.7 kilograms	2,005.004	209.826	2,529.659
Mincemeat, 46.7 kilograms	20.548	17.279	89.197
Corn meal, 23.6 kilograms	2.124	31.152	108.088
Hominy, 4.1 kilograms	.574	8.036	29.028
Flour, crackers, and macaroni, 330.6 kilograms	92.568	87.956	714.096
Graham flour, 7.3 kilograms	2.701	10.950	48.180
Oatmeal, 26.8 kilograms	20.904	67.732	261.032
Rice, 1.8 kilograms	.216	1.080	3.564
Bread and doughnuts, 20.1 kilograms	4.221	3.819	32.562
Cornstarch, 3.2 kilograms	....	....	....
Tapioca, 0.9 kilogram	....	....	....
Sugar, 226.8 kilograms	....	....	....
Molasses, 102.3 kilograms	363.165	179.848	135.036
Maple sirup, 25.6 kilograms	31.488	25.600	25.600
Beans, 31.7 kilograms	68.155	79.884	348.066
Beets, 67.1 kilograms	12.749	19.459	63.745
Carrots, 3.2 kilograms	2.464	1.024	3.008
Sweet corn, canned, 111.4 kilograms	50.130	77.980	286.298
Lettuce, 3.4 kilograms	1.530	.408	2.482
Parsnips, 45.4 kilograms	34.504	19.976	83.082
Peas, 6.4 kilograms	8.768	13.056	54.720
Peas, canned, 41.5 kilograms	9.545	14.110	58.930
Potatoes, 445.9 kilograms	71.394	178.360	642.096
Potatoes, cooked, 6.4 kilograms	1.229	3.070	11.059
Pumpkins, canned, 10 kilograms	3.200	1.400	1.350
Squash, 58 kilograms	1.856	.812	7.830
Squash, canned, 20.4 kilograms	6.523	2.856	27.540
Tomatoes, 46.7 kilograms	8.873	7.472	21.005
Catsup, 12.6 kilograms	2.394	2.016	5.670
Horse-radish, 8.4 kilograms	11.424	3.192	10.668
Apples, 10 kilograms	1.100	1.400	2.600
Apples, dried, 19 kilograms	7.030	10.260	22.990
Apricots, 22.7 kilograms	4.767	4.313	13.166
Bananas, 12.7 kilograms	1.143	4.445	7.747
Blackberries, canned, 10 kilograms	5.200	2.300	5.500
Blueberries, canned, 10 kilograms	3.000	1.000	3.100
Lemons, 6.8 kilograms	4.284	5.712	13.776
Prunes, 6.8 kilograms	4.284	5.712	13.872
Raisins, 4.5 kilograms	1.890	3.150	10.800
In total food	3,178.135	1,363.394	9,139.367
In cooked food not eaten and in waste (37 per cent)	1,175.909	504.455	3,381.565
In food eaten	2,002.226	858.939	5,757.802
Per man per day	1.390	.596	3.998

DIETARY CONTAINING CHEAP PROTEIN (NO. 150).[a]

The matron was given the following instructions: Select animal food so far as possible from the following sources: Forequarter of beef, fresh pork, ham, fresh cod, salt cod, and milk. During this period furnish milk as freely as it is called for, three times a day if possible. Furnish beans freely, twice a week regularly if practicable and whenever called for. Plan for such dishes as will require milk in cooking. Make a free use of bread. It is desired in this period to make the relative supply of meats smaller as compared with the bread and vegetables supplied than was the case in the second period.

The study began May 20, 1895, and continued 27 days. Meals eaten by men, 4,454; by women, 334. Total equivalent to 1 man for 1,596 days.

The food eaten furnished 112 grams of protein and 3,620 calories and cost 26 cents per man per day.

The table below shows the kind and amount of foods used, together with the estimated amounts of lime, magnesia, and phosphoric anhydrid furnished by each and by the diet as a whole.

Estimated ash constituents in dietary study No. 150.

Food materials used.	Calcium oxid.	Magnesium oxid.	Phosphorus pentoxid.
	Grams.	*Grams.*	*Grams.*
Meat: Beef and pork (total meat protein, 59.3 kilograms)	45.068	112.670	1,363.900
Fish: Cod and salmon (total fish protein, 25.9 kilograms)	46.620	59.570	725.200
Eggs, 83.9 kilograms	83.900	12.585	307.913
Butter, 116.6 kilograms	25.652	1.166	36.146
Milk, 1,909.6 kilograms	3,284.512	343.728	4,143.832
Corn meal, 33.1 kilograms	2.979	43.692	151.598
Hominy, 4 kilograms	.560	7.840	28.320
Flour and crackers, 457.5 kilograms	128.100	118.950	988.200
Graham flour, 20 kilograms	6.200	30.000	132.000
Oatmeal, 27.2 kilograms	21.216	67.728	264.928
Cake (as bread), 0.9 kilogram; cake, 6.1 kilograms	1.470	1.330	11.340
Cookies, molasses, 3.4 kilograms	1.360	1.020	8.500
Cookies, sugar, 4.7 kilograms	.987	.893	7.614
Pie, apple, 4.5 kilograms	1.350	1.350	4.500
Pie, cream, 2 kilograms	.800	.600	3.000
Pie, custard, 18.1 kilograms	10.860	5.430	36.200
Pie, mince, 5.9 kilograms	2.596	2.183	11.269
Pudding (as bread), 2.7 kilograms	.567	.513	4.374
Cornstarch, 3.2 kilograms			
Chocolate, 1.4 kilograms	1.974	6.762	12.558
Sugar, 248.8 kilograms			
Molasses, 77.3 kilograms	274.415	136.048	102.036
Maple sirup, 42.2 kilograms	51.906	42.200	42.200
Beans, 55.3 kilograms	118.895	139.356	607.194
Beets, 41.7 kilograms	7.923	12.098	39.615
Catsup (as tomatoes), 7.7 kilograms	1.463	1.232	3.465
Greens (dandelions), 14.9 kilograms	9.536	7.897	15.347
Horse-radish, 1.6 kilograms	2.176	.608	2.032
Onions, 4.5 kilograms	1.800	.675	3.600
Parsnips, 2.7 kilograms	2.052	1.188	4.941
Peas, canned, 15.7 kilograms	3.611	5.338	22.294
Potatoes, 433.6 kilograms	69.376	173.440	624.384
Pumpkins, canned, 14.1 kilograms	4.512	1.974	19.035
Rhubarb, 95.3 kilograms	57.180	9.530	98.159
Squash, canned, 10.9 kilograms	3.488	1.526	14.715
Tomatoes, canned, 37.2 kilograms	7.068	5.952	16.740
Turnips, 35.6 kilograms	30.972	10.324	38.092

[a] U. S. Dept. Agr., Office Expt. Stas. Bul. 38, p. 35.

Estimated ash constituents in dietary study No. 150—Continued.

Food materials used.	Calcium oxid.	Magnesium oxid.	Phosphorus pentoxid.
	Grams.	*Grams.*	*Grams.*
Apples, evaporated, 15.9 kilograms	5.883	8.586	19.239
Apricot sauce, 10 kilograms	1.400	1.300	3.900
Bananas, whole, 10.9 kilograms	.981	3.815	6.649
Blueberries, canned, 20.6 kilograms	6.180	2.060	6.386
Lemons, whole, 101.2 kilograms	43.516	16.192	48.576
Pineapple, whole, 21.3 kilograms	8.094	5.751	4.686
Prunes, 6.8 kilograms	4.284	5.712	13.872
Prunes, cooked, 6 kilograms	1.080	1.440	3.660
Raisins, 2.3 kilograms	.966	1.610	5.520
In total food	4,385.528	1,413.857	10,007.729
In cooked food not eaten and in waste (30 per cent)	1,315.658	424.157	3,002.318
In food eaten	3,069.870	989.700	7,005.411
Per man per day	1.923	.620	4.389

DIETARY WITH LIMITED MILK SUPPLY (NO. 151).[a]

In this dietary the meat and vegetable foods were selected as under ordinary conditions and the amount of milk furnished was reduced with a view to determining the effect of a limited milk supply on the amount and cost of the nutrients actually consumed. The study began September 2, 1895, and continued 49 days. Meals taken by men, 10,071; by women, 470. Total equivalent to 1 man for 3,514 days. The food eaten contained 131 grams of protein and 4,595 calories and cost 27 cents per day.

The table below shows the kind and amount of foods used, together with the estimated amounts of lime, magnesia, and phosphoric anhydrid furnished by each and by the diet as a whole.

Estimated ash constituents in dietary study No. 151.

Food materials used.	Calcium oxid.	Magnesium oxid.	Phosphorus pentoxid.
	Grams.	*Grams.*	*Grams.*
Meats: Beef, veal, mutton, pork, poultry (total meat protein, 179.3 kilograms)	136.268	340.670	4,123.900
Fish: Bluefish, cod, halibut, oysters (total fish protein, 24.2 kilograms)	43.560	55.660	677.600
Eggs, 169.4 kilograms	169.400	25.410	621.698
Butter, 235.4 kilograms	51.788	2.354	72.974
Milk, 3,064.1 kilograms	5,280.252	551.538	6,649.097
Cream, 2.3 kilograms	3.381	.345	4.278
Chocolate, 2.7 kilograms	3.807	13.041	24.219
Corn meal, 34 kilograms	3.060	44.880	155.720
Cornstarch, 3.6 kilograms			
Flour, crackers, and macaroni, 1,313.5 kilograms	367.780	341.510	2,837.160
Graham flour, 20.4 kilograms	7.548	30.600	134.640
Hominy, 4.1 kilograms	.574	8.036	29.002
Maple sirup, 15 kilograms	18.450	15.000	15.000
Molasses, 29.9 kilograms	106.145	52.724	39.468
Oatmeal, 106.6 kilograms	83.148	265.434	1,038.284
Rice, 4.5 kilograms	.540	2.700	8.910
Sugar, 557.5 kilograms			
Tapioca, 3.2 kilograms			
Beans, yellow-eyed, 50.8 kilograms	114.808	132.588	627.380

[a] U. S. Dept. Agr., Office Expt. Stas. Bul. 37, p. 40.

Estimated ash constituents in dietary study No. 151—Continued.

Food materials used.	Calcium oxid.	Magnesium oxid.	Phosphorus pentoxid.
	Grams.	*Grams.*	*Grams.*
Beans, white, 39.5 kilograms	84.925	99.540	433.710
Beets, 25.9 kilograms	4.921	7.511	24.605
Cabbage, 117.9 kilograms	68.382	24.759	95.499
Carrots, 3.6 kilograms	2.772	1.152	3.384
Cucumbers, 15.9 kilograms	4.452	2.862	8.268
Onions, 17.2 kilograms	6.880	2.580	13.760
Potatoes, 1,481 kilograms	236.960	592.400	2,132.640
Sweet potatoes, 247.2 kilograms	61.800	46.968	197.760
Pumpkin, canned, 15.9 kilograms	5.088	2.226	21.465
Squash, canned, 1.4 kilograms	.448	.196	1.890
Squash, 10.4 kilograms	3.328	1.456	1.404
Sweet corn, fresh, 18.1 kilograms	8.145	12.670	46.517
Sweet corn, canned, 27.4 kilograms	12.330	19.180	70.418
Tomatoes, 190.3 kilograms	36.157	30.448	85.635
Turnips, 47.6 kilograms	41.412	13.805	50.932
Cucumber pickles, 22.2 kilograms	6.216	3.996	11.544
Horse-radish, evaporated, 0.18 kilogram	.244	.068	.228
Horse-radish, fresh, 2.95 kilograms	4.012	1.121	3.746
Catsup, 6.8 kilograms	1.292	1.088	3.060
Apples, 680.4 kilograms	74.544	95.256	176.904
Bananas, 56.7 kilograms	5.103	19.845	34.587
Blackberries, 34 kilograms	26.860	12.580	28.220
Blueberries, 30.4 kilograms	13.680	4.560	13.984
Crab apples, canned, 11.6 kilograms	.812	1.044	1.972
Cranberries, 13.6 kilograms	2.856	1.632	4.624
Currants, dried, 4.5 kilograms	7.605	3.420	8.110
Pineapple, canned, 5 kilograms	1.250	.900	.700
Prunes, 9.1 kilograms	5.733	7.644	18.564
Raisins, 7.7 kilograms	3.234	5.390	18.480
In total food	7,122.250	2,898.787	20,571.960
In cooked food not eaten and in waste (19 per cent)	1,353.227	550.769	3,908.672
In food eaten	5,769.023	2,348.018	16,663.288
Per man per day	1.461	.668	4.741

DIETARY WITH LARGE AMOUNT OF MILK (NO. 152).[a]

Meat and vegetable foods were selected as under ordinary conditions and milk was furnished freely with a view to determining the effect on the amount and cost of the nutrients actually consumed. The study began October 21, 1895, and continued 49 days. ·Meals taken by men, 11,083; by women, 470. Total equivalent to 1 man for 3,851 days. The food eaten furnished 120 grams of protein and 3,990 calories at a cost of 25 cents per man per day.

The table following shows the kind and amount of foods used, together with the estimated amounts of lime, magnesia, and phosphoric anhydrid furnished by each and by the diet as a whole.

[a] U. S. Dept. Agr., Office Expt. Stas. Bul. 37, p. 45.

Estimated ash constituents in dietary study No. 152.

Food materials used.	Calcium oxid.	Magnesium oxid.	Phosphorus pentoxid.
	Grams.	*Grams.*	*Grams.*
Meats: Beef, veal, venison, mutton, pork, poultry (total meat protein, 174 kilograms)	132. 240	330. 600	4,002. 000
Fish, etc.: Clams, halibut, oysters, salmon (total fish protein, 20.7 kilograms)	37. 260	47. 610	579. 600
Eggs, 108 kilograms	100. 000	16. 200	396. 360
Butter, 153.3 kilograms	33. 726	1. 533	47. 523
Milk, 4,712 kilograms	8,104. 640	848. 160	10,225. 040
Mincemeat, 7.7 kilograms	3. 388	2. 849	14. 707
Flour, crackers, and macaroni, 996.2 kilograms	278. 936	259. 012	2,151. 792
Graham flour, 30.8 kilograms	11. 396	46. 200	203. 280
Cake, frosted, 2.7 kilograms	. 567	. 513	4. 374
Cake, fruit, 0.7 kilogram	. 147	. 133	1. 134
Cake, sponge, 10 kilograms	2. 100	1. 900	1. 620
Cookies, sugar, 3 kilograms	. 630	. 570	4. 860
Corn meal, 39.5 kilograms	3. 555	62. 140	180. 910
Cornstarch, 22.2 kilograms			
Hominy, 6.8 kilograms	. 952	13. 328	48. 144
Maple sirup, 25 kilograms	50. 184	40. 800	40. 800
Molasses, 25 kilograms	88. 750	44. 000	33. 000
Oatmeal, 86.2 kilograms	67. 236	214. 638	839. 588
Rice, 2.3 kilograms	. 276	1. 380	4. 554
Sugar, 502.1 kilograms			
Tapioca, 6.8 kilograms			
Pie, apple, 9.1 kilograms	2. 730	2. 730	9. 100
Pie, cream, 5.9 kilograms	2. 360	1. 770	8. 850
Beans, dried, 98.3 kilograms	211. 345	247. 716	1,079. 334
Beans, string, 57.2 kilograms	41. 756	28. 600	52. 052
Beets, 16.3 kilograms	3. 097	4. 727	15. 485
Cabbage, 37.2 kilograms	21. 576	7. 812	30. 132
Carrots, 9.1 kilograms	7. 007	2. 912	8. 554
Celery, 4.5 kilograms	4. 230	1. 215	4. 500
Horse-radish, dried, 1.3 kilograms	1. 768	. 494	1. 651
Onions, 27.2 kilograms	10. 880	4. 080	21. 760
Peas, canned, 44.9 kilograms	10. 327	15. 266	63. 758
Peas, dried, 38.9 kilograms	53. 293	79. 356	332. 595
Cucumber pickles, 27.2 kilograms	7. 616	4. 896	14. 144
Potatoes, 1,193.4 kilograms	190. 944	477. 360	1,718. 496
Sweet potatoes, 63.5 kilograms	15. 875	12. 065	50. 800
Pumpkin, canned, 25.9 kilograms	8. 288	3. 626	34. 965
Squash, canned, 10.9 kilograms; squash, fresh, 67.1 kilograms	24. 960	10. 920	105. 300
Tomatoes, canned and catsup, 56.3 kilograms	10. 697	9. 008	25. 335
Apples, 547.5 kilograms	60. 225	76. 650	142. 350
Apple sauce, 5 kilograms	. 350	. 450	. 850
Apricots, dried, 19.05 kilograms	186. 690	169. 545	518. 160
Bananas, 39 kilograms	3. 510	13. 650	23. 790
Blueberries, canned, 5.4 kilograms	14. 700	4. 900	15. 190
Cranberries, 5.4 kilograms	1. 134	. 648	1. 836
Currants, dried, 5.4 kilograms	9. 126	4. 104	9. 612
*G*rapes, 18.6 kilograms	2. 604	3. 534	12. 090
Currant jelly, 29 kilograms	9. 280	4. 930	13. 630
Prunes, 34 kilograms	21. 420	28. 560	69. 360
Raisins, 24 kilograms	10. 080	16. 800	57. 600
In total food purchased	9,871. 851	3,169. 790	23,219. 565
In cooked food not eaten and in waste (19 per cent)	1,875. 651	602. 260	4,411. 717
In food eaten	7,996. 200	2,567. 530	18,807. 848
Per man per day	2. 076	. 666	4. 883

It will be seen that in all of these dietaries milk was quite freely used as compared with food habits the country over, and the amounts of lime and magnesia were liberal in all cases and the amount of phosphorus appears to be entirely adequate in view of the fact that all of the subjects were grown.

It is, however, a very noticeable fact and one of great importance to practical dietetics that, in these experiments made under perfectly normal conditions on a large scale and with no reference (at the time) to the ash constituents of the food, the most expensive dietary furnished the smallest amounts of each of the three ash constituents here studied. This is in accordance with the present general tendency to rate as of especially high quality foods which are either naturally poor in ash or have been "refined" to such an extent as to largely deprive them of their natural ash constituents. The most conspicnous examples are to be found among the foods of vegetable origin, such as refined sugar and starch, polished rice, and similar foods. It is therefore of especial interest to note that in this case the selection of the more expensive animal foods tends also to result in a lowering of the desirable ash constituents of the dietary.

Comparing the amount of lime per man per day in the different dietaries of this series it will be seen that in both cases on changing from a more expensive dietary to a less expensive one containing more milk there was an increase of over 25 per cent in the amount of lime furnished per man per day. The amount of magnesium was not noticeably affected by the change in either case, and the phosphorus was in one case increased and in the other decreased by something less than 10 per cent. It is chiefly in the calcium content, therefore, that the dietary was improved when a part of the more expensive proteid foods was replaced by a more liberal supply of milk.

An experimental dietary study (No. 486)[a] upon an individual subject. made in connection with the study of iron in food and nutrition, may also be noted here. The primary object of this study was to determine whether it is feasible to obtain a palatable and satisfactory diet rich in iron without the use of meat, eggs, or the more expensive fruits and vegetables, and without employing unusual articles or combinations of food.

The cost as compared with that of family dietaries under like conditions was very moderate. The iron content which has been discussed in detail in a previous bulletin was high. From the data given in the accompanying table it will be seen that the amounts of calcium, magnesia, and phosphorus were also largely increased over those found in most of the family dietaries selected for discussion in this bulletin.

The study was made during fourteen days of January, 1906. The food eaten furnished 100 grams of protein and 3,188 calories at a cost of 27.8 cents per day.

The table below shows the kinds and amounts of foods used, together with the estimated amounts of lime, magnesia, and phosphoric anhydrid furnished by each and by the diet as a whole.

---

a U. S. Dept. Agr., Office Expt. Stas. Bul. 185, p. 62.

227

Estimated ash constituents in dietary study No. 486.

Food material and weight of edible portion.	Calcium oxid.	Magnesium oxid.	Phosphorus pentoxid.
	Grams.	*Grams.*	*Grams.*
Milk, 15,196 grams	26.137	2.735	32.975
Butter, 300 grams	.066	.003	.093
Lard and pork, clear fat, 497 grams			
Bread ("entire wheat") 3,315 grams	2.718	2.652	9.249
Crackers, 310 grams	.086	.080	.669
Wheat breakfast food, 1,545 grams	.664	3.692	14.615
Beans, peas, dried, 680 grams	1.462	1.713	7.466
Potatoes, 1,195 grams	.191	.478	1.720
Vegetable soup, condensed, canned, 625 grams	.162	.131	.663
Apples, evaporated, 215 grams	.079	.116	.260
Bananas, 895 grams	.080	.313	.545
Prunes, 400 grams	.252	.336	.816
Raisins, 1,335 grams	.560	.934	3.204
Peanuts, 365 grams	.229	1.036	.686
In total food eaten	32.686	14.219	72.961
Per man per day	2.33	1.02	5.21

From the results of all of these experimental dietaries it may safely be said to have been demonstrated that the desirable ash constituents can readily be increased by proper selection of food materials without decreasing the attractiveness or increasing the cost of the dietary.

CONCLUSION.

To facilitate comparison of the ash constituents of American dietaries with each other and with the protein content, the results of the work described above upon 20 typical dietaries are brought together in the following table, in which the studies are arranged in order of the amounts of protein consumed per man per day:

Comparative summary of ash constituents in typical dietaries—Quantities per man per day.

Dietary study No.	Persons studied.	Fuel value.	Protein.	Iron (Fe).	Phosphoric acid.	Calcium oxid.	Magnesium oxid.
		Calories.	*Grams.*	*Gram.*	*Grams.*	*Grams.*	*Grams.*
391	Maine lumbermen	6,780	179	0.035	5.88	1.27	1.21
91	School superintendent's family, Chicago	3,260	123	.021	3.97	1.09	.55
207	Students' club, University of Tennessee	3,595	123	.019	4.05	1.22	.63
190	Decorator's family, Pittsburg	3,305	112	.019	3.44	.90	.48
45	Farmer's family, Connecticut	3,545	108	.021	3.53	1.15	.55
44	Teacher's family, Indiana	2,780	106	.016	3.64	1.42	.44
485	Teacher's family, New York City	3,180	102	.017	3.92	1.69	.54
181	Mechanic's family, Tennessee	4,060	97	.017	3.58	.90	.72
182	Farmer's and mechanic's family, Tennessee	2,820	95	.019	3.56	.83	.59
191	Glassblower's family, Pittsburg	3,085	94	.016	2.73	.49	.36
43	Lawyer's family, Pittsburg	3,280	91	.015	2.82	.83	.40
323	Women students' club, Ohio	3,330	85	.015	2.88	.97	.67
112	Laborer's family, New York City	2,335	84	.014	2.41	.47	.30
128	Laborer's family, Pittsburg	2,525	83	.013	2.40	.50	.34
139	Negro farmer's family, Alabama	4,955	80	.012	3.25	.21	.74
129	Laborer's family, Pittsburg	2,440	77	.012	1.52	.40	.19
35	Laborer's family, New York City	2,430	71	.012	2.27	.50	.29
208	Farm students' club, Tennessee	3,560	66	.011	2.08	.46	.34
48	Sewing woman's family, New York City	1,500	54	.009	1.84	.68	.23
100	Very poor negro family, Alabama	2,240	44	.007	2.05	.08	.52

It will be seen from this table, as has been pointed out in a previous bulletin, that the amounts of iron in the different dietaries are approximately proportional to the amounts of protein. In a general way, and so far as it goes, this observation tends to confirm the common assumption that a diet containing liberal amounts of protein is likely to furnish at the same time liberal, or at least adequate, amounts of iron. Evidently, however, it can not be assumed that liberal quantities of protein involve adequate amounts of all of the ash constituents. As a rule the dietaries rich in protein are also fairly high in phosphoric acid, but the parallel is not nearly so close here as in the case of protein and iron. With calcium and magnesium the discrepancies are greater, and it can hardly be said that the amounts of these elements run even approximately parallel to the amounts of protein in the twenty dietary studies which have been compared and which are believed to be fairly representative of the food habits of people of at least the eastern half of the United States. In view of these figures it can no longer be assumed that the amount of protein in a dietary is a sufficient measure of its richness in "building material." Aside from nitrogen, the elements of "building material" which appear to require special attention in dietaries are iron, phosphorus, and calcium.

The occurrence and distribution of iron in foods, its functions in nutrition, and the question of iron supply in dietaries, has been discussed in another bulletin. The outline above given of the distribution and functions of phosphorous and calcium compounds, while of necessity incomplete, is yet sufficient to show the great importance of these compounds in the nutritive processes and to emphasize the necessity for adequate supplies in the food.

Of the various classes of phosphorous compounds found in food, the organic combinations appear in general to be of greater nutritive value than the inorganic forms, and it is probably for this reason that different experiments indicate quite different amounts of phosphorus as necessary for the maintenance of equilibrium in man. From the results here obtained, as well as from the average results of experiments by other observers, it would appear that a healthy man, accustomed to full diet of the ordinary mixture of animal and vegetable food materials, requires for the maintenance of his ordinary store of phosphorous compounds about 1.5 grams of phosphorus, or nearly 3.5 grams of phosphoric acid, per day, though under special conditions or with a specially selected dietary equilibrium may be maintained on much less. Many of the dietary studies show so much less than 3.5 grams of phosphoric acid per man per day as to raise a question whether these people may not have been undernourished in this respect, even though they may have had ample proteins, fats, and carbohydrates. This question merits further investigation.

227

Little is known regarding the form in which calcium exists in food materials, and at present differentiation among the different groups of calcium compounds eaten can not be made. Metabolism experiments indicate that a healthy man accustomed to full diet requires about 0.7 gram of calcium oxid for equilibrium, but many of the dietaries show less than 0.7 gram calcium oxid per man per day. Gautier in France and Albu and Neuberg in Germany hold that the food should furnish at least 1 to 1.5 grams calcium oxid per man per day. If these estimates of the normal requirement and the estimates of the amounts in typical American family dietaries are even approximately correct, it would follow that a considerable proportion of American families would be benefited by food richer in calcium compounds than that which they habitually consume. This subject calls for much more extended study, especially in view of the fact that recent medical observations are tending to show that disturbances of calcium metabolism are connected with a number of abnormal conditions.

Experimental dietary studies have shown that it is entirely feasible to increase largely the calcium and phosphorus intake by making a more liberal use of milk in the dietary. The same may, of course, be said of the various milk products in which the calcium and phosphorus compounds are largely or wholly retained, such, for example, as cheese, junket, kumiss, buttermilk, or cream. This is probably the simplest and more effective means of improving the dietary as regards calcium and phosphorus compounds, without decreasing its acceptability or materially increasing its cost and with distinct advantages in other directions.

The progress of research during the four years which have elapsed since the above-described experiments were performed and most of the foregoing text was written has still further emphasized the importance of calcium and phosphorus in food and nutrition.

227

O